Secrets Within Us

A.M. McCoy

Contents

Warnings   V

For Us   VII

1. Chapter 1 - Hadley   1

2. Chapter 2 - Kip   7

3. Chapter 3 - Hadley   25

4. Chapter 4 - Kip   49

5. Chapter 5 - Hadley   61

6. Chapter 6 - Kip   89

7. Chapter 7- Hadley   103

8. Chapter 8 - Kip   117

9. Chapter 9 - Hadley   129

10. Chapter 10 – Kip   153

11. Chapter 11 - Hadley   159

12. Chapter 12 - Kip   185

13. Chapter 13 - Hadley   199

14. Chapter 14 - Hadley   215

15. Chapter 15 - Kip   231

16. Chapter 16 - Hadley   243

17. Chapter 17- Kip   253

18. Chapter 18 - Hadley   273

19. Epilogue – Kip   279

20. Epilogue – Hadley   291

Warnings

As with all of my books, there are elements that may be disturbing to readers. To protect your mental health, please visit my website at ammccoybooks.com to view them. If you have any questions at all, please don't hesitate to reach out to me at ammccoybooks.info@gmail.com.

For Us

This book is for every reader who has ever had to have a healing journey, no matter the cause. Healing isn't linear, it isn't one size fits all, and it does not care what other's opinions are of its timeline. Embrace your journey and know that you are never alone in it.

You have me.

Chapter 1 - Hadley

Cold

C old.

It was so cold. The tormenting kind of cold that settled into my bones so efficiently, that I suddenly found myself not cold at all.

And that was when I knew it was time to panic.

Yet I couldn't rouse the energy to worry, not even a little. Everything I had left inside of me went into picking up my feet and placing them one step ahead of the other in the snow.

When had it started snowing?

Shit, that wasn't good. I was losing my grip on reality; I could feel it slowly slipping from me as the icy wind blew the branches around in the trees above me.

I needed to get out of the cold, but no matter where I looked, all I saw was forest and snow. It closed in on me from every side.

The sun had gone down hours ago, I no longer had any way of knowing what direction I was walking in. I could go in circles, and I wouldn't know it because the falling flakes were filling in my tracks faster than I could make them.

I grabbed the lapels of my jacket to pull it closer to my body, trying desperately to ward off the ice as it spit from the sky. The zipper on my jacket had long ago broken, and I'd never in a million years thought I'd be using the cheap brand to ward off the frigid temperatures of a forest. Being trapped in the freezing depths of hell wasn't on my bingo card for the year, or else I would have bought another one before I left.

I hadn't known I'd be needing it; I was on my way to Florida where I should have been watching the sunset from the sandy beach with my toes in the ocean.

The knee-deep snow was definitely not the ocean, and there was definitely no warmth shining down on me.

Everything inside of me hurt, every muscle, every bone, every fiber. I had little strength left to keep going, but I knew if I stopped moving, I'd die.

I came up to a low branch in my way and rather than walk around it, expelling more energy than I could afford, I tried to step over it. My feet and legs, numb from the cold, caused me to clumsily catch it instead of clearing it. My sides screamed in pain as I lurched forward, falling face-first into the powdery hell. The pain of my broken ribs and beaten body paled compared to the excruciating pain I felt as my hand connected with hard metal on the ground. I didn't have a second to think before the metal folded in on itself, locking my hand in the razor-sharp teeth of an animal trap chained to the branch I fell over.

The sound that escaped my throat was a scream, so horrifying and otherworldly, it seemed to vibrate through the naked branches of the winter-kissed trees. An involuntary gasp escaped my lips as I instinctively jerked my hand away from the searing pain. Unfortunately, my suffering only intensified as the trap became entangled in the chains. The flesh and bone of my hand ripped with the jarring motion, eliciting another gut-wrenching scream from my lips.

I had screamed way too many times over the last six days; more than the rest of my twenty-three years combined. My throat burned with the strain as I continued to wail into the dark emptiness of the forest.

I crouched down in the snow next to the trap, careful not to disturb it anymore than I'd already done as I tried to control my breathing. The glistening metal teeth of the trap became covered in blood as it poured from my flesh.

I tried to open the trap, but it was impossible with only one free hand, and my efforts resulted only in the teeth digging further into my skin. "Fuck!" I screamed to the treetops as I cried and tried to come up with a plan to get free.

I couldn't tell if the blood coating both hands was from the gruesome wounds I had just inflicted on my-self or from the day before.

Was it my blood?

Or was it his?

Falling to my bottom in the snow, my energy once again waned, and the adrenaline retracted from my nerves.

I sat there in the snow for hours, trying to get my hand free. Without both hands and with little strength left in my body after living in captivity and walking all day and night, I couldn't make it budge. I had a small duffle bag of clothes next to me, but there wasn't anything in there that would help me. The sun started creeping over the surrounding hills when I finally accepted defeat and laid back in the snow. It was all too much. I'd been through too much the last few days. I couldn't take it anymore.

Laying there, feeling the wet cold snow soak into my back and shoulders, having lost feeling completely in my lower extremities from sitting on the ground hours ago, the numbness began to burn. I felt a sort of calm lay over me like a blanket as I drifted into idyllic blackness.

I'd come so close to getting away; to winning. I'd overcome so much to have it end in the bitter loneliness of defeat.

He had won.

I had lost.

And no one would ever know what really happened to me on that mountain now that both of us were dead.

Chapter 2 - Kip

L ying in bed, I tried to sleep off yet another alcohol-induced stupor when a piercing scream woke me out of a dead sleep. I froze, staying as still as possible, trying to quiet any noise as I strained my ears to hear it again from my bedroom.

I stopped breathing completely, waiting for it to prove to myself that it wasn't my mind playing tricks on me. Living in silence and solitude like I did, could make a man second guess his gut after long enough. Even someone like me with the particular set of skills I possessed.

But then, on the next gust of wind, that shrill scream found me again through the walls of my cabin.

I swung my feet from my bed and into my boots in one swift motion, one that came from muscle memory after years of repetition. Even though hours ago I'd hardly been able to crawl up the stairs to my bed. Crossing the room, I pulled my flannel on as I headed towards the stairs. When my boots hit the wood floor downstairs, Endeavor, my giant Cane Corso dog, stood by the door waiting for me already.

I quickly had my sidearm holstered and my jacket on, as I grabbed my rifle and threw the door open.

Dev shot off the porch with his nose to the ground as I paused at the edge, listening again for that pained wail.

I was confident it was a human scream, not an animal, though I could have been wrong. The wind was whipping around me, covering me with snow rapidly as the storm raged on overhead.

Dev stopped sniffing and tuned his ears in as he looked around. He was trying frantically to figure out the direction it came from. Once more, the echoed pain pierced the air, but it reverberated off all the trees around me as I tried to pinpoint a direction or even a distance.

But it was impossible.

The storm was too strong to be sure of anything. I looked over at Endeavor as he stared back at me, but even his ears couldn't pinpoint where the noise came from.

"We can't chance it boy, we could both get killed in the storm and we don't even know which way to go." I sighed, slumping back into the house, leaving the front door open for him to follow when he was ready.

I shucked off my now completely covered outer clothes and walked over to the large fireplace to throw a few more logs on as the fog of the whiskey fell back over my mind and the adrenaline slowed down in my veins.

Who would be out in the storm so strong? There were no other houses or even camps within a twenty-mile radius, which was why I chose the property to isolate myself from the world and avoid interacting with anyone. Yet someone had tried to face off with Mother Nature. And by the time I got out there at first light, they'd be a popsicle.

If the bears and wolves didn't get to them first.

Dev came back in shortly after me and curled up by the fire as I shut and locked the front door once more before leaning back in my recliner. I stayed out of bed in case something else happened before morning. I wanted to be ready in case there was a chance to help the poor soul.

After laying there for hours, listening for more screams, sleep pulled me under aided by the liquor I drank. Because the night was silent, and the screams had stopped.

There was one thing I'd learned in my disastrous life; the silence could be more deafening than a scream.

I woke again before the first light as I always did and readied myself and Endeavor for the hike to find what made those awful screams. The snow had stopped sometime around five and as we crossed the buried ground, Endeavor quickly put his nose to work, trying to differentiate any of the surrounding scents. The wind was blowing in from the east all night and given that I heard the screams when the wind blew; I figured that was the direction they came from.

So we headed east, Endeavor and I were on a mission like the old days. The days before my entire world had imploded and ended.

We walked in silence for about two miles, Dev in the lead, both of our heads on a swivel. At one point, he stopped dead in his tracks before quickly turning back to look at me and he took off to his right at a full run, with his nose to the ground still.

"Dev! Slow down!" When he showed no sign of stopping, I took off after him as carefully as I could while still trying to keep my eyes peeled on the horizon. Predators lurked throughout the woods, and given the time of year, the cold starvation would make them do anything for their next meal.

I watched as my best friend ran down a dip in the terrain and grimaced as it took him out of my line of sight. "Dev!"

I sprinted up over the knoll, skidding to a stop when I came across him again, frozen in place. Almost completely invisible to the untrained eye, a pile of snow laid out of place against the flat ground. I knew the storm did not create the pile as it was in the exact spot where I had set up a snare a couple of days ago, between two logs.

Whatever kind of animal got stuck in it was big enough that it should have been able to muscle its way out, but it hadn't. And now, it lay dead on the ground where the storm had buried it with snow overnight.

I quietly squared my body off to the pile as I took the safety off my rifle. If it wasn't dead yet, me coming up on it may spook it enough to make it attack, and while it was smaller than me, it was still probably dangerous. Perhaps a large bobcat, or wolf. If it was a bear, it was a yearling, but even then, it could still do serious damage to me if it got the chance.

"Dev, heel." I quietly commanded, trying my best to keep my voice low. But for the first time since he was just a puppy, my faithful companion disobeyed me and edged closer to the pile. "Endeavor, no. Come!" I gritted out authoritatively, while also praying he would listen.

But of course, he didn't.

He looked back at me quickly before sniffing and walking even closer to the pile. He cautiously sniffed it, gently touching the new snow with the tip of his nose before emitting a pained whimper as he raised his paw to uncover the creature.

I drew my rifle level with the pile, anticipating it to jump up and lunge for my dog, but it didn't move. Endeavor cleared some snow off his side of the pile before letting out a loud bark and looking up at me expectantly. He dug at the animal earnestly, using both his paws and gigantic body to push the snow off it.

I was looking, but couldn't believe what I was seeing. It wasn't fur that he had started

to uncover, but a jacket and jeans.

"Dear God." I cursed and dashed over to Dev as I realized the snow-covered object was a person. The snow had accumulated so much that the body was much smaller than what I'd originally thought. I muttered out loud, "Please, don't be dead," as I removed my gloves and carefully flipped the body from its side to its back. At that moment, I gasped as all the air was sucked right out of my lungs.

A woman lay on the ground before me, buried beneath a foot or more of snow. Her dark hair, matted and frozen, clung to her face and hood as I tried my best to move it and see her face. Bruises and cuts covered her face.

My military training came back to the forefront of my brain, even after years of lying dormant, and I assessed the rest of her body as quickly as I could. Her skin had a blue tinge from the cold, and as I pulled her jacket apart at her throat to check for a pulse, I noticed she was wearing only thin clothing underneath. Her clothing was not suitable for a fall-time stroll in the south, let alone a brutal winter here in the mountains. I stared at her chest and lips, waiting to feel her heartbeat.

I saw nothing but faintly felt a pulse along her jugular. Dropping my ear down to her face, I checked for life escaping her lips.

Dev whined from his side impatiently as he laid down along her, putting his big blockhead across her chest, trying to warm her up. At that moment, I could hear the heavy exhale of air coming from her chest as she strained under the weight of his head resting on her.

"She's breathing! Let's go!" I yelled. As I tried to scoop her into my arms, I noticed her hand and all the blood that colored the surrounding snow.

My trap.

Shit!

How the fuck did she get her hand trapped in the snare? Without a doubt, it was her screams I'd heard last night. Her screams pierced the air as the metal of my trap twisted into her hand, rendering her helpless and alone in the frigid snow where she would have frozen to death had I not heard her.

Despite her being alive, the possibility of death still loomed over her.

Because of me.

I quickly and as gently as I could released the trap from her hand before taking the bandana off from around my neck to wrap around it. It wasn't actively bleeding, but I couldn't let her lose any more blood or strength on the journey back to my cabin. As I wrapped it tightly, a soft moan slipped from her lips, laced with pain as a slight frown creased her brow before fading completely. There was a small bag next to her I scooped up and threw over my back for the journey.

"I'm sorry, stay with me now. I'll get you warm in just a minute."

Lifting her into my arms, adjusting her body to support her head against my chest, tucked under my chin, I whistled for Dev, "Let's go, boy." He was already tromping on ahead, back towards the cabin.

From my long career as a Marine and my time in the northern woods living off the land, I had become accustomed to carrying heavy gear long distances, so I quickly covered the distance between the snare and the warmth of my home.

When I got inside, I laid the girl down on the couch and quickly began ridding myself of my outer clothes and boots.

I watched her intently as I did so, waiting for any movement or noise to escape her body to prove she was still alive. But she just laid there across my couch, motionless and silent. When I was dry, I threw more wood on the fire before carefully taking her thin jacket off her shoulders, careful not to jostle her any more than I needed to.

I wasn't used to handling such a small woman; my large, calloused hands easily dwarfed her small limbs. She was the size of a teenager, but one look at her curves told me she was mature beyond those years, though my guess was not by much. Once I got rid of her jacket, her thin short-sleeved shirt left a lot of blue-hued skin bare to my eyes and the warm air of my home. The sight of her blue, cold skin was alarming enough, but the harsh bruises on her arms and chest added to the concern. They were angry-looking and covered nearly every inch of her skin.

"What happened to you, *bambina*?" I whispered softly before I realized what I'd called her. My grandfather always called my grandmother *Bambina*. It meant little girl in Italian.

She was younger than him and when they had first met; he thought she was an annoying little girl from the neighborhood, even though she persisted and worked her way into his heart over the years. He fondly continued to call her that throughout their marriage, in his way to remind her she was young at heart and small and feminine in his arms.

I shook off the memory and the fondness inside of me and went back to the task at hand. Regardless of what I thought of her, she needed to get out of the clothes she was wearing and into warm dry ones or she didn't stand a chance.

As I carefully removed her clothes, I uncovered a multitude of bruises and contusions, revealing the extent of her injuries. I tried to concentrate on the logical reason that I was stripping her clothes off, but even beneath the bruises, blood, and dirt, she was beautiful.

Gorgeous even.

Her body curved and filled out in the ways an old pin-up model did in such a feminine and lush way. She was incredible to look at and as I took her soaked bra off and slid her panties down; I had to bite back the groan that threatened to rip from my chest at the sight of her bare skin.

My cock grew painfully erect in my pants as I sat there for a moment and gazed down at her.

Dev's sudden bark echoed through the room, causing me to jump and bringing me back to the present moment. He caught me ogling her and called me out on it in his own way.

I felt like such a fucking pervert.

Fuck.

I *was* such a fucking pervert.

She was lying on my couch, hardly alive, and here I was staring down at her naked body that was built after that of a goddess, with a raging hard-on, thinking about how good it would feel to sink myself deep into her plush little body.

Fuck!

It had been way too long since I'd been with a woman, and my predicament was not helping. And it sure wasn't helping her.

I quickly snatched the throw blanket from the back of the couch and tenderly wrapped it around her body. Then, I lifted her up in my arms, trying to ignore the sensation of her warm breath tickling my neck or the way her curves fit perfectly in my arms. I shook my head again and made quick work of the stairs leading up to the loft bedroom above the living area. It was further from the fire, but the heat rose, and my bed had heavy blankets to warm her up quickly.

As I sat down on the bed, I held her up against my body as I pulled down the bedding to make room for her in the center. I took my long-sleeved shirt off the end of the bed and slid it on over her head before pulling it down and covering up her beautiful body.

She had to be in incredible pain, and the jostling I was doing was no doubt increasing her agony, but it needed to be done. Her head lolled to the side as I moved her again. She groaned as her head jarred and her face contorted in pain when I adjusted her with my hands on her sides, over the top of her ribs.

"Shh, I'm sorry. Let me get you settled, and the pain will end."

Her icy fingers fell to my thigh, below the hem of my shorts, and the contrast between my overly warm skin and her ice-coldness caused us both to shiver.

She moaned again and mumbled something as I slid her limp body under the sheets and blankets, bringing them up to right below her chin. Her icy hair began dripping on the pillow as the heat thawed the clumps free.

Filled with worry, I swiftly gathered a clean towel and a complete set of first aid supplies from the bathroom, eager to return to her side before she woke up feeling frightened and all by herself. But when I got back up to the bed, she lay there as still and silent as when I left her.

Her hand was my first priority to tend to, given it was an open wound. It was gnarly looking, but from where the teeth entered; I didn't think it was broken. I wouldn't know for sure until she woke up and tried moving it, though. So I cleaned and wrapped it and then simply watched her, waiting for her to wake up.

I sat there on the edge of my bed, gazing down at her for hours before I moved again. The pink color returned to her skin as she warmed up under the blankets in my bed and I let myself relax a little with each improvement. She slept peacefully all day with me just sitting there watching over her, unable to get up and walk away.

As the sun started setting in the sky outside of the loft windows, I lifted the blankets, placing my hand on her bare leg to see if her skin was warming up as it should be, while also checking her toes for signs of frostbite.

Her head turned to the side on the pillow, like she was searching for where the hand on her was coming from, a soft crease between her brows formed in confusion.

"Mmh." Soft as a whisper, the moan slipped through her lips when my hand moved back up her calf, gently tracing the lines of her leg until I reached her knee. The gentleman in me made me stop right above the joint when to be honest, I wanted to do anything but.

The only noise in the room was my breathing, it had turned ragged and labored the second my fingers contacted her flesh. Her body had such an effect on mine, and I couldn't explain why, because she wasn't even awake.

"Warm. You're so warm." She moaned louder, her voice cracked as she spoke for the first time, as she reached her good hand out and placed it on my hand on her thigh.

I couldn't look away.

I was going to hell for it.

When I looked up at her face, her eyes were open.

I could have drowned in them right then and there and died a happy man. They were so different from the ones I'd fallen in love with all those years ago. Those eyes so long ago had been clear blue, they looked like the depths of the ocean on a sunny day. Yet the eyes staring back at me were incredibly dark green. In the low light, her eyes nearly glowed, fanned by dark sultry lashes. The flecks of gold in her iris' matched the gold and auburn freckles on her cheeks and nose.

Everything about the woman differed from my Molly.

Every. Single. Thing.

And I couldn't figure out why I was so attracted to her despite them.

My hand stilled on her body as our eyes stayed locked on one another.

At first, I thought my touch alarmed her, but I quickly realized she was still disoriented, and she showed no fear when she found my hand wrapped around her thigh.

Neither of us said anything as she slowly came out of the fog and detached her fingers from between mine and laid her hand across her stomach, which was fluttering with rapid breaths. Her eyes left mine briefly to look around the room before landing on mine again.

"Where am I?" Her voice, rough and scratchy, trembled as she asked the question. Beneath the hoarseness, I could hear the honey of it though, and felt my cock pulse in my shorts. The motion caught her eye, and she looked down at the large bulge tenting the fabric.

Finally, her eyes widened with panic, and she glanced back up at me one last time.

Chapter 3 - Hadley

Stranger

here was I?

The giant lumberjack sitting next to me on the bed didn't answer or move an inch at my question. Well, all but one part of him stayed still. I saw movement in his lap and peeked to see his erection under his shorts twitch at my voice. It was then I realized his hand was heavy on my thigh.

What the hell happened before I woke up?

Feeling the alarms ringing through my system, I instinctively closed my legs slightly, causing him to jolt and release his grip on my thigh as if snapping out of a trance.

He cleared his throat before he pulled the heavy blanket up to cover me. When I attempted to free my arms from under the blankets, a sudden jolt of pain ran through my hand and up my wrist, causing me to let out a hiss.

He quickly folded the blanket back and cradled my hand in his as he pulled it out to sit on top of my stomach.

The trap. I remembered giving up hope of getting the trap off. Did he get it off?

"Shh, easy. I can get you something for the pain now that you're awake, but it'll put you back to sleep." The powerful vibrations of his deep voice surrounded me, which filled me with a pleasant, tingling warmth. He seemed so incredibly large, filling up every inch of air around me, but for some reason, I didn't fear him. Which was so fucked up, in reality. I didn't think a man his size had it in him to be gentle at all. But there he was, nurturing and being gentle and kind.

"Where am I?" I asked again and watched as his entire demeanor changed again, morphing into something guarded.

"My house." He answered with his back to me as he simply walked from the room without a parting word.

"But where is that?" I yelled out after him as he descended the stairs quickly. I could hear him walking around downstairs, the railing along the room at the end of the bed led me to believe it was a loft with living space below. The combination of pine walls, ceiling, and steel furniture created a rugged and masculine atmosphere.

The bed I was in smelled masculine as well. Not in a cologne way but in a fresh air and woods way. Exactly how he smelled when I got a whiff of him as he leaned over me to stand up.

I was in his bed.

His.

The lumberjack.

He was tall, I noticed when he left the room. Probably six feet and a couple of inches. His body was ripped with muscles from his jaw to his feet. He wore basketball shorts and a flannel shirt, but didn't have any socks on. He had striking dark features, with his dark hair, a rugged looking almost black beard, and piercing dark brown eyes.

Brooding like.

Which meant I wasn't doing myself any favors by laying in his bed completely defenseless, waiting for him to return, so I got up, at least if I was on my feet, I'd be more alert.

When I tugged the blankets off, I discovered all I had on was a baggy, long-sleeved shirt that didn't fit me properly. Perhaps his?

It didn't matter though, because when I saw the bruises marring my bare legs, all the memories of the last few days flooded back at once like a dam let loose.

Every slap.

Every punch.

Every kick.

Every sadistic word grunted into my ear while he was on top of me.

Every moment spent in the freezing cold.

My body looked like it went through war and back in one day flat. And that was exactly how I felt laying there. Moving was necessary. I had to keep moving.

Pulling myself up by the blanket to sit with my feet dangling off the tall bed, I tried to force the world to stop spinning. Finally, when it did, I slid down to the plush carpet, enjoying the sensation of my toes sliding through it.

I looked around the room for my clothes, but they were nowhere to be found. The shirt I was wearing went down to my knees, meaning it would have to be enough because I needed to get out of the bedroom.

Survive, Hadley. You've come too far to lose now.

As I descended the stairs, I noticed that the wall across the living space below consisted entirely of windows that overlooked the forest.

Trees and snow surrounded the house I was in. It did not differ from the entire last week of my life. The very landscape that nearly killed me the last time I escaped surrounded me.

Did I need to escape this place like I did the last? How long had I been here? Was I in danger here too?

I didn't stand around contemplating it any longer, though. I put one foot in front of the other as I made my way down the stairs, one step at a time. Every movement made me nearly scream out in pain, I had to wrap my arms around my middle and mash my teeth together to keep silent.

When I got to the bottom step, I looked around the open floor plan of the living space distractedly.

It was beautiful.

Elegant and whimsical, reminding me of a cozy cottage in the woods you'd find in a fairy tale. Was the roof covered in thatch, with white puffy smoke billowing from the stone chimney? What a pleasant change it'd be to find myself on the good end of a sweet fairytale instead of trapped in the horrific nightmare I'd been in.

I put my foot out to step off the last stair as the mysterious man came around the corner with a pill bottle and a wet washcloth in his hands.

"What are you doing out of bed?" The sheer force of his tone startled me, making my hands tremble and my grip on the banister loosen. Unable to maintain my balance, I sank to my knees, the hardness of the tile floor jarring against my skin.

As soon as I landed on the floor, a massive black animal pounced towards me, making me scream and instinctively raise my hand to protect myself from its looming attack.

"Dev, heel!" The lumberjack bellowed from across the room, causing the animal to stop mid-stride before sitting down and looking back at the man.

It was a dog.

Sweet Jesus, a big fucking dog. But a dog, nonetheless.

Inhaling sharply, I watched as the lumberjack advanced towards me, his footsteps reverberating against the hard floor, and then the agony seared through me as I fell to the unforgiving ground. I sagged forward on my good hand, keeping my bad one wrapped around my stomach, trying to hold my ribs in place as I fought hard not to cry.

The man fell to his knees in front of me and quickly slid his fingers through my messy hair to push it out of my face, cupping the back of my neck as he searched my face. "Are you okay?"

The sobs threatened to spill out of my mouth, but my locked jaw held them back. I managed a brief nod; all the while trying to calm my breathing and ease the intense pain in my ribs.

"That dog is massive," I whispered, finally catching my breath as I sat down on the bottom step, feeling the pain pulsating through my body. I kept my eye on the giant animal, even though the lumberjack was between us.

He looked so menacing, just like his owner.

"You don't have to worry; he won't hurt you. He's the one who found you, so I think he's actually pretty fond of you already." The man said as he held out his hand to help me up. "You really shouldn't be walking around right now, you're too injured and too weak." He was still squatting in front of me on the floor, his face even with mine as I sat there.

He looked sincere as he said it, but there was something else there too, buried under his gaze. Almost as if he was annoyed that I was too weak to even walk. And that thought instantly pissed me off.

So I grabbed the railing and, as gently as I could, pulled myself up to stand, blatantly ignoring his offer for help as I did. As I watched, his brow furrowed even more, revealing his growing irritation at being snubbed.

Yeah well, I didn't appreciate the disdain, big guy.

"For two days, I walked in the forest in sub-freezing temperatures. I can handle walking around this house." I spat out.

He stood up then, instantly towering over me once again. "Two days?" He asked incredulously. "I'm surprised you survived the night, let alone two days." Grimacing at me, he cast a disdainful glance at my small, hunched-over frame. "How did you get out here, anyway? I found you miles from any road or house, there isn't anything around these parts. But somehow you ended up buried under the snow, with your hand stuck in a trap, wearing clothes better suited for spring," His eyes drifted down my body once more, taking in my bare legs under the hem of his shirt that I was wearing.

The path his eyes took left a warmth across my skin like he had caressed me with his hands again. "And your entire body looks like it went through ten rounds with a grizzly," he said, his eyes widening in disbelief. "So, do me a favor and explain how you ended up on my property like you did."

"Not until you answer some of my questions." I raised my nose defiantly at him, not able to give an inch. If he thought I was being rude, so be it. It was better than him knowing the truth.

He huffed as he stepped back and motioned for me to sit in the armchair next to the fire. I didn't want him to know it, but I was incredibly grateful for the reprieve from standing on my battered legs and craved the warmth of the flame. As I hobbled over, he took a blanket off the back of the chair and draped it over my legs before sitting on the coffee table in front of me, leaning with his elbows on his knees.

"What do you want to know?" He said curtly.

I opened my mouth to start, but he stopped me quickly by putting his hand up. "Know that for every question you ask, you answer one and that there is an expiration date on me humoring you with answers."

As he nodded for me to start, a wave of uncertainty washed over me, leaving me unsure of what questions to ask. I couldn't answer his questions, of that I was sure. Even so, I needed some answers, so I figured I'd ask only super essential ones.

"Where are we?"

He answered with no hesitation. "I told you already. My house. You were on my property when I found you."

"No, I mean where, though. What town? What—state?"

He just stared back at me for a second before leaning further forward. "How do you not know what state you're in right now?"

I had to tread carefully right now. I didn't know if he was friend or foe yet and couldn't risk telling someone too much. "Answer me first."

He took a deep breath and watched me intently as he stated. "Utah. Outside of Provo, south of Salt Lake."

"Utah," I whispered as I tried to wrap my head around it while not giving anything away on my face. My gaze fell from his as the reality of that made my world spin again.

"What happened to you?" He asked quietly. His voice took on a calm, gentle edge I hadn't heard yet, and his face relaxed with sincerity.

But I couldn't tell him.

I had to take it to the grave.

And that grave had already been dug for me.

So instead I lied. "I don't know."

"You're lying." He answered instantly.

I didn't look back up into his eyes as I stated. "That's not a question. Or an answer to one."

"Fine. Why are you lying, then?" When I didn't answer or look at him again, he tipped my chin up with his fingers until my eyes met his. "Tell me what happened to you or tell me why you won't be honest."

"I don't know how to answer that." He looked ready to interject again, so I held my hand up between us, "Truthfully. I don't know what happened to me exactly. I don't—understand it. Therefore, I can't answer you with anything other than I don't know right now."

He mulled that over again as he dropped his hand back to his own knee. "But someone did this to you?" He asked as he waved his hand toward my battered body. "It wasn't a car accident or something, right? Someone put their hands on you and beat you to a bloody fucking pulp, right?"

"Yes," I answered quietly again and dropped my gaze to my hands folded in my lap.

"Was it your boyfriend? Or an ex?" He asked rapidly, trying to make sense of everything.

"You're not letting me ask questions," I said to cut him off.

He took a deep breath before rubbing his hand over his face exasperatedly, and then sat back and nodded for me to proceed.

"No, it wasn't a current or past boyfriend." He nodded again, then, just one curt nod, like he already knew the answer to that.

"I don't take you for the kind of girl to let a man beat up on her regularly and I don't take you for the kind of girl to date someone who would try."

"You're right, I'm not and I wouldn't. But enough about me for a second. I don't even know your name."

He hesitated briefly, deciding if he would answer. "Kip. You?"

"Hadley." I didn't give my last name, seeing as how he didn't.

"How old are you?" He asked quickly as he looked back over my body again, as if he was trying to tell how old I was by that alone.

"Twenty-three. Yourself?" I pulled the blanket up to cover my chest a little as his eyes settled there, no doubt having an easy view of my breasts through the thin shirt. They weren't small, leaving them hard to hide without a proper bra or baggy sweatshirt.

He noticed my moves, and no doubt knew why I was doing it, realizing that he had been caught. "Thirty-five." He stood up and walked over to the fire and put another log on it and I welcomed the heat.

He grabbed a bottle of water out of the fridge and walked back over to me with it, holding out a pill in his hand for me to take as well.

I took the water, but eyed the pill suspiciously. "What is it?"

He chuckled slightly, showing laugh lines around his eyes quickly before his face settled back into the somber gaze he was so frequently sporting. "Do you think I'd drug you? I already had you unconscious in my bed, had I wanted to do anything to you, I could have done it then." He paused like he was waiting for me to tell him I didn't think he would do that, but I couldn't give him that. "It's Vicodin, probably going to make you groggy, but it will help with the pain."

I had to trust the man because he was my only lifeline. I had no alternative but to trust the man, and I was ready to do almost anything for relief from the suffering. Swallowing the pill with a gulp of water, I sank back into the chair, wrapped in the cozy blanket and basking in the warmth emanating from the crackling fire. However, I remained vigilant, observing his every move as he busied himself around the house, signaling the end of our Q&A session.

My tired voice cut through the silence of the house, startling him slightly as he was preparing food for dinner. "How do I get home from here? I don't have any money or my phone or anything. I had a bag of clothes with me when I was walking, I think. But that's it." My stomach had been growling non-stop since he started grilling meat on the stovetop twenty minutes ago, but I didn't know if he intended to feed me or not. It wasn't like he had to.

He kept working as he answered. "The storm that's been pounding down on us for two days currently blocks the only way into town. It will take a couple of days for the plows to get up here after the snow stops.

You're too weak to make the trip by snowmobile and I doubt your ribs would let you ride at all, anyway. So we wait for the snow to stop and the plows to clear the road and then we'll head into town in my truck. There's a landline here, but it's hit or miss in a storm like this. You're more than welcome to use it to check in with your family or friends when it works, let them know you're okay."

I nodded my head like I agreed. But the truth was, I had no one to call. No family. Not a single friend. Not even a boss or coworker to call to say I wouldn't be at work today or tomorrow.

I had no one anymore. The man here, the lumberjack named Kip, was the only human being to know I was alive right now. And he had no idea what power he held over me because of it, either.

I didn't have long to ponder it though, because he brought me a plate of grilled chicken, mashed potatoes, and biscuits where I sat in the chair. He set a tray up on my lap, asking if it hurt anything being there, before putting my plate on it and adding a napkin and a glass of milk. I couldn't remember the last time someone served me a meal.

Maybe never. Emotions burned in my chest as his hospitality warmed a small part of my frigid heart.

I waited until he settled himself across from me in his recliner with a similar tray and meal before I thanked him.

"Thank you." I sounded weak and tired, but I didn't have the energy to get mad at that right now. The pain medication had been effective, but it left me feeling even more drained as if my body had become an anchor.

Kip looked up at me from under his lashes as he cut into his chicken as if he were contemplating what to reply with. Like someone hadn't thanked him for anything in a long time. And perhaps nobody had, there was no one around but me and his dog.

He curtly nodded his head at me as he took a large bite of his food. I neatly cut into my meal, getting only a few bites down before it felt like I was too tired to even lift my arms to feed myself. I ate much slower than Kip, and he quickly cleared his plate and got up, reaching for mine understandingly.

"You'll have more energy and be capable of doing more tomorrow." I just nodded as he put the food away before feeding his monster, Endeavor, or Dev, as he called him.

"Where can I sleep?"

He didn't stop moving around the room as he answered, turning off lights as he got closer to me. "In my bed. You need the best sleep you can get to heal quickly, and that's the comfiest spot in the house." He handed me another pill and opened the bottle of water for me from the stand next to the chair. "Take this, it will help you sleep."

I wasn't sure why I was just doing what he told me to do, but I quickly took the pill, feeling the stab of pain slowly creeping back into my body. I picked up the blanket and went to stand, but Kip was faster than me. "Let me." He gently slid his hands under my knees and around my back, effortlessly and gently lifting me into his arms against his chest as he walked towards the stairs. His bare arms were warm against the skin of my legs where he held me.

What caught me off guard was that his touch didn't incinerate fear into my soul, in stark contrast to the terror I felt with the monster before him. Instead, something else burned low in my belly, something that resembled arousal.

But that was crazy.

"I, uh, I need the restroom... please." I stammered, desperate to get out of his arms and onto my own feet again.

How freaking embarrassing.

Kip turned directions, saying nothing, and went to the back of the cabin into a spacious updated bathroom. He gently set me on my feet on the cold tile, but when he let go, my legs were shaky, and I had trouble stabilizing myself. I couldn't tell if it was from my injuries or from the effect he had on me.

With a rapid motion, he clutched my hips, being mindful not to cause any discomfort to my ribs, and deftly spun me around, effectively pinning me against the counter. I rested my hands on his stomach as I fought to keep my head upright and from falling into his broad chest like I so badly wanted to.

He was just so strong and steady. So opposite of me.

"I'm sorry. I've got it now." With embarrassment, I struggled to untangle my hands from his shirt, which was tightly clinging to his rock-hard abdomen.

"Just take it easy. Go slow. I'll leave the door open, and I'll be right down the hall, just holler if you need anything." I shook my head, letting him know I was capable, but he did as he said, anyway. Leaving the door open and going back out to the kitchen.

When he left, I quickly hobbled to the toilet, relieving myself, and then returned to the counter before he walked back in. However, when I reached the vanity, I suddenly lost all focus and didn't mind the lack of privacy he had left me. I looked up and caught a glimpse of myself in the mirror above the sink.

My hair was a rat's nest, hanging off my head at awkward angles. Both eyes were black and blue, and multiple cuts and bruises covered my cheeks and lips. Bruises encircled my neck, stretching all the way to my collarbones, hidden from sight by my shirt. I was almost glad I couldn't see them.

Pushing my hair off my shoulder, I turned my head slightly, noting how the bruises around my neck were in the shape of a hand.

His hand.

Kip stood silently behind me at the door, watching me in the mirror as I assessed myself. The scowl returned to his face, his brow furrowing deeply as he watched.

Tears pooled in my eyes at the pathetic image I'd become. I looked nothing like the strong, independent woman I'd fought so hard to become over the last few years. Gently pressing my fingertips to my lips in horror at what *he* had reduced me to.

Kip moved forward to stand behind me in the mirror. "I know you said for now you can't tell me what happened. But I need to know if you're in danger anymore. If someone could be after you, following you here. I can't protect you if you don't let me know what I'm up against." Although he didn't touch me at all, I could feel the warmth of his body radiating into mine. He stood so much taller than me, my head only came to the middle of his chest, and his broad shoulders flanked my much smaller ones on each side.

A single fat tear broke the barrier of my eyelashes, rolling slowly down my battered cheek before falling into the fabric of the shirt at my chest. I shook my head softly as I locked eyes with him over my head. "No one is coming for me. Neither good nor bad. There's no one out there to care if I'm alive or dead." I didn't wait for his reply, instead, I gingerly walked out of the bathroom, using the counter and walls for support. I felt him near behind me, turning off the lights as we went, leaving us shrouded in only the warm glow from the fireplace in the living room as I put my foot on the bottom step of the stairs.

I didn't get very far before he wrapped his arms around me once more, lifting me into them effortlessly.

"Thank you," I whispered against his neck as I settled my head against his shoulder.

"Don't thank me, I'm only doing it because if you walked ahead of me up the stairs, I would have been too tempted to look up the bottom of the shirt you're wearing. It's safer for me to not be tempted."

Pulling my head off his shoulder, I looked at his face to gauge his seriousness, but I should have known better because Kip was only ever serious.

I swallowed quickly at his admission. "I meant for everything, not just for carrying me. For saving me and letting me impose on you until you can take me into town. Thank you for all of it. You could have left me out there."

He said nothing as we reached the top of the stairs and entered his bedroom again. He knelt down on the bed and laid me gently on the opposite side of it against the comfortable pillows.

"Are you cold?" He asked gruffly, his kindness once again covered and marred by his social awkwardness.

I was cold but didn't want to impose on him further, so I just silently shook my head no.

He nodded once again before standing back up off the bed. I thought he would leave, but to my astonishment, he made it as far as the chair in the corner. With his back facing me, he nonchalantly yanked his shirt off over his head using the back of the collar. I drank in the sight of his wide back, covered in thick ropes of muscles and dark swirls of ink. Tattoos covered every inch of his back, and as he dropped his arms and set his shirt on the chair, I could see that his entire right arm was covered as well.

My jaw dropped as I lay there, completely captivated by his presence. He turned around, his eyes meeting mine, and a sly smile crept onto his face as if he had expected my rapt attention. I quickly dropped my eyes to my lap as my face heated with a furious blush.

With a coy gaze, I watched him as he reached for the drawstring on his shorts, swiftly untying them and then sliding them off his hips until they gathered on the floor. He stood in only a tight pair of black boxer briefs for a second before he turned back towards the bed, hitting the switch on the wall for the overhead light as he went.

I watched in confusion as the bedside lamp illuminated every ridge and dip of his washboard abs and delicious chest as he stalked silently. His chest and abdomen were covered in tattoos and seeing all that darkness matched with his dark personality left me nearly panting and slightly scared of him.

He pulled the blankets back on the other side of the bed and adjusted the pillow before crawling in next to me. I must have looked alarmed because he once again looked over his shoulder at me, smirking as he reached and turned off the light.

"There's only one bed in this house, Hadley. And I'm sure as hell not sleeping in the recliner again tonight. Just go to sleep, I have no intentions of doing anything other than sleeping tonight."

He lay flat on his back, looking up at the ceiling with an arm slung over his head and the other resting between us in the bed. The bed was queen-sized, but with both of us in it, it felt no bigger than a twin.

Too soon.

It was too soon for me.

I didn't know him; he could be a bad person.

"Go to sleep *bambina*, you're safe here." He breathed into the darkness as if he could hear my fear through the air.

I rolled over, placing my back towards him, and laid there for a while, spinning every bad-case scenario through my head before the pain medication took effect and pulled me under the serenity of slumber.

But *he* chased me through my dreams relentlessly.

Not the man in plaid with a scowl so fierce it made his smiles earth-shattering, but the man who smiled constantly, making his scowls even more terrifying than the pain he inflicted while wearing them.

Chapter 4 - Kip
One Bed

Her breathing evened off shortly after she rolled over, the pain medication no doubt pulling her under and away from her thoughts. She was so troubled; I could almost see her thoughts every time I looked over at her while she sat next to the fire.

She told me she didn't know what happened to her, but that it was someone. And when she looked at herself in the mirror, the emotional pain was obvious all over her tiny, perfect face.

Even through the bruises and cuts, she was perfect. It made my chest ache with an unrealistic need to tear apart whoever hurt her. Someone, a man more than likely, beat her almost to death and then left her out in the freezing cold to die.

Who would do something like that? She said it wasn't an ex or a boyfriend. But who else would attack someone as small as her? It was almost inhumane to think about how unmatched that fight must have been. Especially around here, the town was tiny, everyone knew everyone else, and I couldn't think of one person who would want to hurt her. Not a single person.

I looked over at her, huddled under the blankets, so incredibly tiny next to me, so helpless and vulnerable. But I could tell she didn't live her life helpless or vulnerable. She was calculating and confident. In her normal life, she probably controlled everything she could as best as she could because there were so many things she physically couldn't have the upper hand in.

Just then, she turned in her sleep towards me, slowly and easily scooting closer to me until she was curled around my arm between us.

Shit.

She was like an adorable, loveable puppy that I just didn't want. Every time I was short or curt with her today, I could see the rejection and pain on her face until she just stopped trying to interact with me at all.

The sooner the roads cleared, and I got her into town and back on her way home, wherever that was, the better. There was a void inside me, leaving no energy to foster feelings for her or to extend my concern beyond her overall wellness.

I just couldn't. It wasn't fair to *them*.

She didn't deserve my affection or kindness; she hadn't earned them like they had.

I raised both arms up over my head on top of my pillow to eliminate the contact she initiated. Resigning myself to a sleepless night, when she moved in closer again, probably just seeking my warmth.

She was still sleeping, mewling quietly as she moved closer. She settled her head on my shoulder before curling her body around my stomach and legs, effectively wrapping herself around me like a tiny cat.

I stared at the ceiling as she settled completely after giving out a contented sigh into my neck.

I should have pushed her away, I contemplated it multiple times as I lay there being lulled by the steady puffs of breath coming from her lips against my chest. But instead of doing what my head was telling me to do, I did what my body was telling me to do. I brought my left arm down, wrapping it around her back, laying my large hand on her tiny hip as I tried to ignore how well her petite body fit against mine in such a foreign way.

She wasn't at all like Molly.

My soulmate, the love of my life.

The only one I wanted to spend the rest of my life with.

Opposite my wife, the little curvy pixie next to me in my bed was completely different. My wife was tall and leggy, with blonde hair and clear blue eyes. Molly was my equal in every way; she was physically strong and capable, never needing me to do anything for her that she couldn't. She always found a way. And she was always a rock, holding our home together while I was away constantly.

Having the pixie in my bed was a slap in the face to my incredible wife. Even as innocent as I intended it to be. But as I had mentioned earlier, it was best for me to avoid temptation.

"Shit," I murmured quietly, guilt and hate washed over me for the millionth time since I'd laid eyes on Hadley's angelic face early that morning.

"Please don't be mad at me. I didn't mean to make you mad." Hadley pleaded from her spot on my chest.

I looked down at her face to see she was still fast asleep, talking through a dream, perhaps. Her small hand came up to my chest, her short nails digging into the skin as she fought some internal battle in her head.

I gently slid her off my shoulder, replacing it with her pillow as I sat on the edge of the bed. I needed to be careful with her. She was way too much of a mystery to me, I couldn't chance anything happening between us.

"Fucking hell," I muttered into the dark again as the images of her naked in my living room rushed back into my head. I knew I should get up and put distance between us, but I couldn't get my body to move away from her.

"Is something wrong? Did I keep you awake?" I heard her soft voice, barely audible, coming from behind me. She leaned up on her elbow as I glanced over my shoulder. The shirt she was wearing had slid down off her shoulder, showing off her delicate collarbone and dainty neck. Her bright green eyes glowed in the dark as she let her gaze rove over my back and side.

Lust shined through the darkness as her eyes snapped back up to mine.

"You're a bed hog," I said harshly. Instantly regretting it, her eyes dropped to the sheets in embarrassment. Shame burned in my stomach.

"I'm sorry, I'm not used to sleeping next to someone. I'll just go downstairs." She gently raised herself up and started scooting to her side of the bed again to get out.

"Stop," I commanded, turning back towards her. But she didn't stop moving towards the edge.

"No, it's fine. I'm sorry for disturbing you, I'll just go sleep in the chair." She continued.

"Stop," I said more aggressively as I leaned across the bed and grabbed her elbow. She said she wasn't used to sleeping next to anyone, so that must mean she was single and had been for a while. That information shouldn't have excited me, but it did. "It's fine, just lay back down. It's an adjustment for both of us." I pulled her arm back until she laid down flat on her back, but not before I saw her shiver from her toes to her teeth. "Are you cold?" I carefully pulled the blanket up and over her bare legs, ensuring she was warm before I turned to lie on my side, my eyes locked on her.

I propped my elbow on the pillow and put my head on my hand as I looked down at her, waiting for her to answer. She wouldn't meet my eyes but nodded her head.

"Vocalize what you need from me so I can fix it for you," I stated plainly, but she looked back up at me like I'd just spoken Greek to her. Like me, fixing her problems was so absurd. Looking back on my observations and conversations with her, I realized she probably wasn't familiar with people extending a helping hand. She didn't have anyone to lean on, no one to sleep next to, no one to care that she was alive or dead, as she'd said earlier.

She was all alone.

Except for me, now.

"Roll over," I said gruffly, to which she responded with a pensive questioning glare. "I'm just claiming my share of the mattress now, so hopefully you'll stay on your side." Placing my hand on her hip, I nudged her, encouraging her to roll on her side, facing away from me. "I'll get you warm in no time, then we can both go to sleep."

Slipping my arm under her pillow and positioning it in the crook of her neck, I pressed my large body against hers, bending my legs to make sure that mine embraced every inch of her skin.

When I felt her soft curves perfectly molding against my hard body, I couldn't help but curse myself. At first, she stiffened against my hold, but within a few moments, she took a deep breath and relaxed. I slid my hand under the blankets to rest on her hip, knowing her ribs were in too much pain to lay my beefy arm across them. The shirt she was wearing had ridden up and my fingers skimmed the bare skin of her hip. They quickly, of their own accord, slid higher, taking the shirt with them and finding the crease where her hip met her thigh and into the soft skin there before settling.

We both lay silent, our breathing more labored than probably necessary. Her presence in my bed brought a newfound sense of comfort and contentment as our bodies intertwined in a tender embrace. Even though everything inside of me told me how wrong it was.

"What does that word mean?" She asked softly after a minute.

"What word?"

"*Bambina.*"

I lay silently for a second, trying to think of an appropriate answer, "It means nothing."

She huffed lightly, clearly annoyed by my dismissive response to her question.

"You're lying." I could hear the indignation in her voice as she accused me softly in the dark. She didn't raise her voice though, in fact, every time she spoke to me it was soft and melodic, almost like a kid's fairy tale character. Almost like the fairy tale princesses in the kids' movies, I used to get sucked into watching. The ones where the fair maidens had birds and woodland creatures following them around everywhere they went, singing. But she wasn't some innocent beauty frolicking through my forest, she had darkness surrounding her and it had kissed her skin over and over again, leaving her marked.

"You would know all about lying to someone's questions now, wouldn't you?" I replied because, well, I was a bastard, and I just couldn't leave well enough alone.

I felt her sharp intake of breath and knew that was an asshole thing to say, but I couldn't take it back because not knowing exactly what happened to her still didn't sit well with me. It went against everything I'd ever trained for and prided myself on being about.

She said nothing else and after a while; I felt her fall asleep, and I drifted off to the rhythmic pattern of her slow breathing.

When I woke up again, I was disoriented and confused. Bright mid-morning sun shone through the windows across from the loft and it hurt my eyes as I tried to acclimate to my surroundings. Not in years had I ever woken up after the sun was fully up.

My body and head were working at two different speeds, the way it does after an extremely deep hard sleep. When I finally remembered myself, I looked to my left to check for Hadley but found the bed empty and cold.

"Hadley!" I yelled as I swung my feet to the floor and took off to the stairs.

What if she robbed me blind and took off with my dog and truck?

Okay, that sounded like a country song.

But I knew nothing about her and her mysterious appearance on my property left more questions than answers.

I made it downstairs without falling on my face in my haste, hitting the hardwood with a loud thud as I looked around the living space for her. The heavenly scent coming from the kitchen should have knocked me on my ass if gravity didn't, but I'd been too frantic to pick up on it at first. She stood there, with her hair up in a messy bun, still wearing only my long-sleeved shirt, rolled up her arms a dozen times to clear her wrists, and my slippers from by the front door that I hardly ever wore.

"Good Morning." She said shyly from behind the stovetop on the island as she flipped through a couple of pieces of sausage.

"Morning," I answered curtly, trying to figure out why finding her standing in my kitchen wearing my shirt left me feeling relieved and incredibly aroused.

"I hope you don't mind; I was starving and didn't want to wake you." She said as she gestured to the sausage in the pan and the fresh biscuits warming on the plate next to the gravy.

"You made biscuits and gravy?" I tried to hold back any harshness in my tone. She nodded shyly again, making eye contact only for a brief second at a time. "From scratch?"

"Yeah, you had everything for the biscuits in your pantry and the sausage was in the freezer." She shrugged. "I whipped the gravy up from the two of them. I figured I should at least cook and clean for you while I'm here. Try to earn my keep, even if it's still short by a long shot from what I owe you."

"You don't owe me anything, Hadley," the harshness was back in my voice, and she dropped her gaze again to the pan. I wasn't mad because she was cooking, I was mad because she thought she needed to cook to stay. "But I won't turn away good home cooking." I tried to soften my obvious lack of tact and good manners by accepting her offer.

She paused briefly, "Well, wait until you try it to tell me if it's good or not." She answered with a coy smile as she looked up shyly from under her lashes, and even just a half smile as it was, it lit up her entire face.

No, the entire room.

She was breathtaking.

She had two deep dimples that formed when she smiled, and she completely shook my world upside down with them.

"I was just kidding, I'm a pretty good cook. You won't get sick from it, I promise." She said, her smile dropping self-consciously as I stood there staring at her like an idiot.

I shook my head, snapping myself out of it. "Yeah, no I got it. Let me get dressed and I'll be right back."

And with that, I walked out, trying even harder to get a grasp on myself.

Chapter 5 - Hadley

He disappeared upstairs, shaking his head like I'd confused him.

He was the most frustrating man I'd ever met.

He was the confusing one!

I got all the food off the stove and onto plates, carefully carrying them to the table, trying hard not to drop them from my weakness as I replayed our conversation in my head, looking for clues about the mysterious man. When he came back down, he was in jeans and a fleece pullover. He stopped and let Dev out the front door on his way to the table, staying completely silent and unreadable.

"I didn't know what you wanted to drink, but there's fresh coffee in the pot if you'd like some." I babbled stupidly.

Of course, he knew where the coffee was; it was his house after all.

My subconscious was a real self-loathing bitch some-times.

"Sit down and eat Hadley, I'll grab some coffee and be there in a second." I cautiously lowered myself onto the chair at the small wooden table, as if his words some-how granted me permission.

He came out of the kitchen and sat across from me, instantly digging into his meal without caution. Even if I were the worst cook in the world, he bravely took a massive bite, risking an unpleasant taste.

He looked up, catching me staring at him quizzical-ly as he chewed, before he grinned lopsidedly as he swallowed. It should be against the law for a man as good-looking as him, to scowl so frequently and smile so rarely. "It tastes great, thanks for cooking. But you don't have to do anything. You should be resting."

"I can handle it. I would, however, like to use your shower after breakfast if it's not too much trouble." Pausing briefly, "Oh yeah, did you find a bag of my clothes when you found me?"

"Yeah, I placed them in the laundry room when I brought you in because they were wet from the snow, and I wanted them to dry for you. They should be all set by now."

"Thanks." Once again, he finished eating before I did and quickly took care of the plates once I was done. Just as I was about to tidy up the dishes in the sink, he intercepted and stopped me in my tracks.

"Come on, I'll show you where everything is in the bathroom and then you can shower while I clean up out here. I have to go outside and do some work around the property today, so I'll be gone most of the day. Probably won't be back in until dinnertime." He stared pointedly at me, and I wondered what the shaggy dark hair around his temples felt like. "Just make yourself at home and relax, okay? Don't do anything strenuous, especially if I'm not here in case you hurt yourself." He continued, snapping me out of the mental sexual daydream I had no business having. "There are books all around the living room and quite the movie collection in the entertainment center. Just relax and I'll cook dinner when I get back."

He talked as he walked away down the hallway to the bathroom, so I followed silently. There were three doors at the end of the hall, one was open to the bathroom I'd used last night and this morning, and the other, he opened to a large laundry/ mud room off the back of the house where he grabbed my clothes for me. The last one though, he didn't open or say what was in there, so I figured it was off-limits and didn't ask. But I'd be lying if there weren't red flags flying at my face each time I walked past the closed door.

He showed me where the toiletries and towels were in the bathroom and then excused himself without another word. In my short time with him, I quickly realized that Kip wasn't a talker. He said what he needed to when the urge struck him, but he was more interested in speaking with body language and facial features than words most times.

I listened from the hallway as he got on his boots and gear and left the house, taking Dev with him. Leaving me truly alone in his space.

With my clothes in hand, I hurried to the bathroom and locked the door behind me. I knew that staying still for too long would only invite unwanted thoughts. And I couldn't afford to think, or I'd break down.

I hadn't cried since I'd escaped. A few tears fell last night when I saw the damage done to my face, but that had been just the beginning of a very large tidal wave of emotions that was building inside of me.

So instead I stripped off the shirt Kip had given me and put it in a hamper in the room's corner, turned the hot spray on in the shower, allowing it to get to the perfect temperature before I carefully stepped in.

The hot water cascaded down my body, providing a soothing sensation as I inhaled deeply as if it was the first breath I had taken in a week.

The rich shampoo from the shelf instantly filled the stone shower with Kip's scent as I lathered it into my tangled hair. I leaned my head back, allowing the water to wash it from my scalp, and just breathed him in.

The entire time, memories of other scents wanted to bombard me.

Dirt.

Musty basements.

Leather.

But I sank into my head even deeper than those memories could go and allowed Kip's woodsy scent to consume me. It was the same way his presence settled something inside of me, too. Somehow, that man had soothed my wounds instead of festering them. Which made little sense.

Yet there I was, standing naked and alone in his shower, the scent of his skin when he held me in his bed last night still lingering in my memory. If I tried hard enough, I could almost block out the way it felt when the monster had touched me instead.

But I couldn't use Kip or the bizarre circumstance we'd found ourselves in to distract me from the truth. It would catch up with me someday, I just knew it. Because girls like me didn't get second chances, we weren't born with nine lives and endless opportunities. We were born with wit and an uncrushable will to survive, which got us out of more sticky situations than luck ever did. There were limits, though, and I wouldn't get free unscathed.

I focused on the present as I cleaned myself, but as the washcloth rubbed over the scratches, cuts, and bruises covering my body, I remembered what form of torture *he'd* used to inflict each one.

Which leather belt he snapped.

Which wooden cane he swung.

Which whip he cracked.

Which blade he ran along my skin.

Which position he forced me into so he could force himself inside of me.

That wound, the one inside of me, ached the worst. I couldn't reach the source of its pain deep inside my soul, and no matter how long I scrubbed, I still ached.

I don't know how long I stood there scrubbing my body with soap, but I re-lathered multiple times. Before I knew it, my wounds were reopening and blood was flowing from my scrubbing.

I stood there silently, letting the water run down my body, watching it mix with the crimson ooze as it ran down into the drain.

No matter how many times I scrubbed, the dirt was still there. The emotional dirt. It would always taint my skin. The awful things he did to me would never leave me, even as I washed the blood and grime off.

My weak legs trembled, unable to support me any longer, and I reached out for the side of the stone shower as they gave way completely, causing me to collapse beneath the refreshing spray.

And that's when the dam broke, and the tears fell. I cried forever. Nearly passing out multiple times from hyperventilating and exhaustion. I let it all out, trying to relieve some of the burden on my heart and mind. Using the solitude and the steam to loosen the binds that held it all in. But it wouldn't make it better.

Nothing could make it better.

I had no choice but to move forward as if nothing had happened. I had to survive and crying on the shower floor wouldn't help me at the moment. So I allowed myself one more minute of heartache and weakness. And then I got up.

I turned the cold water off and forced myself to move forward. One step at a time.

Drying off in a daze, taking out a pair of yoga pants, a sports bra, and a zip-up sweater to wear for the day. Until Kip could take me to town and I could finally leave the frozen wasteland, I had no choice but to make do with the few warm items I had packed.

I was supposed to be in Florida, not Utah.

I never should have been so stupid. So naïve.

I forced myself to get dressed in front of the mirror, taking a complete inventory of my injuries as mental payback for my stupidity.

A couple of my ribs were bruised. My hand felt better, so I was pretty sure nothing was broken in it, but the flesh was pretty mangled. The rest were just contusions, burns, and wounds that would heal with time; I hoped. They'd heal and leave a scar as a reminder of what I survived. That was the best-case scenario, at least.

With my hair tamed into a loose braid, I set out on a mission to find some warm socks to protect my feet throughout the day.

I leisurely made my way through Kip's home without him hovering over me, taking in the whole feel of the place for the first time. I could tell that a woman had a hand in decorating the space, even though it was rustic and manly, there was still a decorator's touch to it all.

I wondered pensively if he had a wife or a girlfriend who decorated the place. Was he the type of guy to lie in bed in only briefs, spooning a woman wearing only his shirt if he was committed to someone else? I didn't see a wedding ring on his hand, but he also didn't strike me as the type of guy who would have worn one either.

I tried deciphering some of the ink on his body without being caught last night, but it was useless. There were names on his skin, no doubt, but I couldn't tell what they were or even guess who they were to him.

Great job Had; you're attracted to a man who is probably married.

His wife was probably some crazy hot supermodel away on a photo shoot and I was just some beaten, ugly, frumpy chick who fell onto his property by chance. She'd probably come back home anytime now and find me here and kick me out back into the snow and bitter loneliness.

There was no way he wasn't in a committed relationship, there was just something about the way he
acted, always so protective and watchful, that made
me think he had someone worth protecting out there
somewhere.

So I did what any warm-blooded woman trapped in
a lumber-snack's remote cabin in the woods with no
access to the outside world would do; I spent all day
looking around the living space and his bedroom for
any clues to tell me more about the mystery man named
Kip that held me in his arms all night long like a man
who cared.

But unfortunately, I found nothing.

Natta.

Zip.

Zilch.

There wasn't a single picture or photo album or anything personal in the space. Not an article of clothing or
a memento to show there was someone in his life.

There was, however, an enormous amount of bourbon in a liquor cabinet in the dining room. And in the
garage off the back of the mudroom, there were *a lot* of
empty liquor bottles.

He must spend his free time drinking.

Which was great, really. Super fantastic. Just the type of man I needed to spend my time with.

I selected a book from the shelf he had pointed out earlier and made myself comfortable in the recliner. As the warm afternoon light filled the room through the windows, I pretended I was on a fancy Aspen vacation, rather than on the run. The fiction I was reading was enough to let me escape from my reality for a while.

When I laid the book down after a couple of hours and looked around the room, I realized the peacefulness of the space was something I could easily get used to. New York City didn't have this. There was always noise, even locked away inside your own home, you could always hear someone else living their life around you.

But here, there was only silence.

I walked up to the wall of windows at one point to look out over the property and caught sight of Kip, by a shed splitting wood. He had taken his jacket off and worked in just a flannel and his Carhartt pants.

Mesmerized by his fluid movements, I couldn't tear my eyes away as he swung the axe with a captivating strength. The way his muscles strained against his clothing only intensified my attraction towards him.

I had never found big, muscled men attractive before, as I typically found myself drawn to the clean-cut business suit type I worked with. But there was something about the rugged strength of his body and personality on display that made me want him.

The thought of wanting a man, any man, someone who could overpower me and manipulate me, especially in the aftermath of what happened with that self-proclaimed "saint," sent shivers down my spine.

Saint.

That's what they had called him.

But the God I knew would never let a man like that into His eternal resting place if He knew what I knew about him.

I bowed my head and prayed as the sun warmed me through the window. I prayed for peace in my head and on my battered body, and I prayed the *saint* would find nothing but flames and pain where he was now.

Pain and flames just like the ones he'd used against me.

I was so consumed by the memories and thoughts waging war in my mind that I never heard Kip come into the house. I stood against the windows still, with the warm blanket from the chair I'd fallen in love with wrapped around my shoulders, watching the sunset over the treetops below when I felt his hand on my shoulder.

Startled by the contact, I instinctively leaped into the air, crying out in pain as my chest and sides throbbed relentlessly. I turned towards Kip in fight-or-flight mode before I realized it was him, then sagged into the window as I fought through the pain.

"I'm sorry," He apologized frantically, "I called your name twice, and you didn't answer. Are you okay?"

I nodded my head quickly as I swallowed back the scream that wanted to rip from my chest.

"Yeah," I croaked. "I'm fine."

"I'm sorry." He repeated as I turned to sit down in the chair by the fire.

"Don't worry about it, I was just lost in thought and didn't hear you."

He nodded curtly, something he did often in response to things like words weren't his go-to.

As I settled into the chair, he disappeared once again, going about his normal routine without another word. Before sitting down on the couch and turning on a movie, he took the time to change into comfortable clothes and prepare a delicious dinner for us. I watched him silently as he filled a rock glass with bourbon and sipped on it while the movie played, though he didn't end up drinking it all. At one point, I looked over at him from my chair and noticed him staring down into the glass, lost in thought, before he looked up at me, locking his gaze with mine until I looked away.

The heat that washed over my body from his stare was enough to leave me sweating. I tried to get back into the movie, but I could feel his eyes on me from where he sat. With the passing of time, I stole a quick glance in his direction, only to find him staring directly at me with an undeniable mix of desire and passion in his eyes.

Despite his usual scowl and brooding disposition, his eyes held a spark of something different as he stared back.

We were transfixed by each other's gaze, while the movie credits slowly rolled in the background. Neither one of us was willing to surrender, even though there was nothing to gain by winning. What was he searching for in my eyes? What did I want to find in his?

There was an intense connection between us, I felt it literally the second I woke up in his bed after he rescued me. But we knew nothing about each other aside from our names and small tidbits we'd discovered through small talk.

But none of it was of consequence.

If he knew me, he'd run for the hills. I was damaged goods, and the look in his eyes indicated that he desired something from me that he would no longer want once he uncovered the whole truth.

And he would find out, eventually. If I stayed with him any longer, he'd work it out of me, or I'd just finally crumble under the weight of it all and tell him. And then he'd make me leave. He'd look at me with disgust instead of lust, and rejection instead of fondness.

And it would break me because, for some reason, he was the first man I ever wanted to think of me fondly.

Back in New York City, I was a paralegal in a prestigious law firm. I worked every single day under the direction and watchful eyes of powerful men who wanted more from me than just my brain.

But I never took that route, regardless of how much easier it would have made my climb up the ladder. I didn't do it because no one there was worthy of having that kind of control over my life.

Yet, sitting in the wicked wilderness that nearly killed me, next to a roaring wood fire, in a beautiful log home, the lumberjack made me feel like I would do anything and everything I could to get his approval and understanding.

I felt like, if I could just surrender the power he so desperately desired, he would protect and provide for me.

But giving him all of that power was too much. I shouldn't do it.

He moved with a gentle ease that mimicked that of a prowling lion as he stood up from the couch. He crossed the distance between us until he was standing in front of my chair, but he still had said nothing. His silence only added to his already infuriating mysteriousness.

He slowly leaned down, resting both hands on the arms of the chair, leaving him nearly face-to-face with me, his mouth just inches from mine. I could see the fullness of his lips under the whiskers of his beard, and I wondered what it would feel like to have them pressed against mine with the furriness in between.

And yet, he still said nothing.

Without looking away from me, he reached over and clicked the lamp off, leaving us blanketed in the darkness of the room apart from the moonlight glowing through the windows.

The shadows played off his features, hiding much of his expression in the dark.

I used to be afraid of the dark.

But I could tell that with him, the dark may prove to be where my soul glowed the brightest.

For the millionth time since I came to find shelter in his home, I found myself drawn to him sexually. I wanted so desperately to lean in and kiss him.

To feel his lips on mine. It was unsettling to realize that I could yearn for that so soon, as if there was a defect in me.

Right?

What was the normal wait time after what I went through for it to be socially acceptable to feel yourself aroused and wanting someone?

Was there a right answer to that?

"You shouldn't want me," I whispered when he didn't move after turning off the light. "You *wouldn't* want me if you knew the truth about me."

There.

I said it.

I gave him an out.

"You shouldn't want me." He said back, his deep voice revealing some emotion other than annoyance and anger for the first time since I met him. "You *wouldn't* want me if you knew the truth about me." He finished, copying what I'd just said to him. "Yet you do. Just like I want you."

He brought his hand up, slowly, off the arm of the chair next to me. I kept my eyes locked on his, even though I couldn't see them clearly through the darkness.

I held my breath as he moved closer to me with a painful calmness. He was never rattled or affected by anything. What I wouldn't give for that same level of control, the ability to hide it all behind a stone mask.

Kip ran his knuckles along my jaw, from my ear to my chin. His eyes dropped from mine to watch the path his fingers traveled, tracing over the bruises that lingered along my skin. They burned under his touch, but not from the pain.

From something more animalistic than that.

He turned his hand, so his calloused fingertips slid down my neck gently before drawing them back up, lifting my chin higher, tilting it towards his.

Goosebumps broke out over my entire body from just the small touches he was giving me. My breaths came rapidly as I tried not to move at all, in fear that he'd stop.

But in reality, that's what I should have been afraid of; him not stopping.

But I wasn't.

He closed the distance between us, bringing his body and face closer to mine until the whiskers of his beard ran across my lips with his breath. I tightly clenched the blanket on my lap, making my knuckles turn white.

"You want me. Don't you?" He asked, his breath warm on my lips. I could smell the bourbon on it and sighed softly at the mixture of the bold liquor and his scent.

For the first time, I didn't question my answer before I gave it. I didn't run all the outcomes and next steps through my head before I found my voice. The old me was brave like that. I needed to be like her again, instead of this wounded and afraid little girl that the monster turned me into.

So I was just honest with him and myself.

"Yes," I whispered.

His jaw locked and his cheek twitched as he swallowed.

But he said nothing else after that. He just closed the distance between us, pressing his warm lips to mine gently.

He pulled away after only a peck but didn't back up, simply detaching his lips from mine. "I shouldn't be doing this." He whispered against my lips as he opened his hand along the side of my face, sliding his fingers into my hair. "I shouldn't *want* to do this." He slid his lips against mine again softly, but only briefly before he licked them with his tongue and sucked my bottom lip into his mouth, where he bit it gently. He was careful of my wounds, but not in a delicate way that mimicked pity. In a caring way, with just the touch of carnal need breathing underneath it, showing me just how badly he wanted to do more.

God, to be desired by a man like Kip.

After everything else.

"Please." I moaned across his lips. But I didn't know what I was begging for.

He pulled my head towards his with more force as he deepened the kiss, growling deep in his throat, sliding his tongue into my mouth as he angled his head to kiss me like his life depended on it.

No one had ever kissed me so deeply, with such rawness. Every other kiss I'd had before that moment felt superficial and shallow. They never left me with the emotions and feelings I got as he dropped his other hand to my thigh.

Even through the blanket, I could feel his warmth against me.

Warm like fire.

Flames.

Pain.

My mind left the room instantly and traveled back to the cell of fear and pain I'd escaped from only days ago.

I felt the panic run up my body from my stomach, into my heart, squeezing off all the air to my lungs.

Kip pushed the blanket to the side as he ran his hand up my thigh again, gentle enough not to hurt me, but with enough bite that I understood his need.

Just breathe, Hadley. I whispered in my mind, reassuring myself.

Kip wasn't evil. Kip wasn't *him*. My desire was the difference between the two situations. And I deserved to desire a man.

I fought to come back to the present, pushing the past out of my mind.

I brought my hands up from my lap, placed them on Kip's shoulders, and slid them around his neck, pulling him in deeper. Sliding my fingers through the hair on the back of his head, he shivered under my touch as he pulled away from the kiss.

He moved down, placing sweet but hot, open-mouthed kisses along my jaw and to my ear. Feeling his hot ragged breath against the shell of my ear left me pressing my thighs together, searching for friction.

"Christ." He cursed as he felt my hips rotate beneath his hands.

"Don't stop," I begged, pulling his face back to mine and attacking his lips once more. I was ravishing him like a horny teenager, and I didn't care. Fuck it all, I wanted him. So damn badly. But more than that, I wanted to want sex to prove I still could.

He didn't stop, instead; he grabbed my hips and stood up, pulling me up with him effortlessly. I instinctively wrapped my arms around his neck while my legs clung tightly to his waist for support.

But then the pain hit from changing positions so quickly and I gasped out, wrapping my arm around my waist as I fought to take a deep breath.

"Ahh." I pulled my lips from his.

"Fuck." He cursed as he gently sat me back down in the chair, kneeling in front of me. "I'm sorry. Shit, I forgot." He apologized profusely, running his hand through his hair in frustration.

I fought through it though, finding that it came easier than it had yesterday to get through the pain.

"It's okay, I'm okay."

He dropped his head, refusing to meet my gaze as he, too, tried to calm his breathing. I could see the walls falling back down over his eyes with each deep breath, though, and I didn't want him to shut me out. Not when he finally let me in, even just this inch. I slid my hands along his scruffy beard to his cheeks, angling his head to look at me again. My hands were tiny compared to his face, and I found it so intriguing. "I asked you not to stop. I forgot about it too until I moved, but I'm fine now."

Yearning for his touch, I leaned back in and pressed my lips against his, silently pleading for him to kiss me again like he had before.

But he pulled his head back again, disconnecting our lips before sitting back on his feet, putting distance between us.

"Don't," I begged pathetically, as I felt his rejection wash over me. He was going to take it back. Bile rose in my throat as that dirty feeling crawled across my skin again like it had in captivity. "Please—"

"I shouldn't have done that-" He started, still not looking at me as I frantically searched his face.

"Don't!" I cut him off. "Don't you dare take it back. You've acted like I've had the plague since I've been here, like I'm the most repulsive woman you've ever met and the second you treat me like an actual human being, you want to take that back? Don't you dare!" I could hear the panic in my voice and knew that my emotions were rooted so much deeper than just our present situation.

He snapped his head back up to me as I called myself repulsive, and shock and remorse tormented his usually stoic face. I knew I was overreacting, and that I was projecting my fears onto him and his rejection, but I couldn't stop it. The words just came out.

We just stared at each other for a million heartbeats in silence before the scowl melted off his face and he said, "Tell me what happened to you."

Then it was my turn to drop my gaze. I looked back down at my lap as I took a deep breath.

Just tell him.

Just tell him about it. Tell someone! Release yourself from the new cell you've locked *yourself* in. My conscience begged me to let someone in for the first time in my life.

I looked up at him where he sat, patiently kneeling.

But I knew so little about him, I couldn't give him that kind of info without knowing him more first. He'd have all the power if I did.

"Tell me what happened to you." My voice was much weaker than I'd intended for it to be. So I took a deep breath and continued. "What happened to you to make you live out here completely alone and miserable? Tell me something that I can hold on to because I obviously can't hold on to you. Your mood swings bring you in and out of my reach every other second."

He stared into my eyes for a moment before shaking his head sadly and sighing as he stood. "That's not how this works. I'm not the one looking for anything or anyone to hold on to, Hadley."

And with that, he turned his back and walked down the hallway towards the bathroom. "I'll sleep on the couch tonight, go on up to bed, you look like crap.

Maybe some sleep will help." He called over his shoulder before shutting the bathroom door.

My chest collapsed as the air left my lungs at his insult.

Of course, he thought I looked like crap.

I just wasn't pretty enough for him, especially without makeup and products. I knew I looked bad with the bruises and cuts, but hearing him say so just shoved my self-esteem further into the ground.

A little mousey, ugly, self-conscious thing like you. No one will miss someone like you, now will they?

I could hear the *saint's* voice like he was in this room with me. Like he was still alive, even. He said such heinous things, hitting them so close to home, like he knew my insecurities without me telling him. I couldn't shake him and his torment.

The sound of the shower turning on broke the stillness of the room, amplifying the cracks in my heart as I sat there in silence and darkness.

I put myself out there, one time.

Just once. Maybe the most important time of my life, too.

And Kip reminded me why I couldn't afford to do that ever again. No one could hurt you when you didn't give them the tools to do so.

I slowly rose to my feet and walked over to his liquor cabinet. Opening it, I grabbed the bottle of top-shelf whiskey I'd noticed earlier and a glass from on top.

I slowly made my way up the stairs, careful not to drop the glass or bottle as each step made the ice in my chest grow thicker and thicker. Endeavor had been sleeping on the couch next to Kip during the movie, but he got up and slowly followed me up the stairs.

I hadn't seen him go upstairs since I'd been there, and I was pretty sure he wasn't supposed to, but I couldn't find it in myself to care.

Frankly, the company would be nice.

So I went upstairs with Kip's large protective dog and his top-shelf whiskey and drank myself into a level of drunkenness that I hadn't achieved since my high school days.

And I finally saw what he found at the bottom of the bottle.

Peace.

Chapter 6 - Kip

Giving In

When I got out of the shower, she was gone. And so was Dev. I heard him walking around in the loft and nearly went up there to get him back downstairs, but couldn't bring myself to face her just yet.

"You win this time, buddy," I muttered quietly as I grabbed a pillow and blanket from the hallway closet.

Kissing her had left me too wound up to just go to sleep. When I'd gotten into the shower, my cock had been rock hard from tasting her and feeling her body under my hands. I'd turned the water to straight cold and hissed out the frustration under the icy stream while I tried to think about anything other than her lips, but my cock still refused to go down at all.

Unable to resist any longer, I turned the faucet and let the warm water wash over me as I retreated into my fantasy, where she played the starring role. Her face had been so small in my hands, but her lips had fit with mine perfectly. When she returned the kiss, her passion and intensity took me by surprise.

My scalp still tingled where she ran her fingernails across the skin, pulling me closer to her.

And as I stood there in the water, my scalp wasn't the only thing tingling at the memory. My cock was rock hard, and my balls were tight and full, and I needed to let loose. I braced one hand on the stone wall and wrapped the other around myself, stroking it quickly in a firm grip before falling into a familiar, pleasurable pace.

I had thought of how good she felt with her ass pressed against my cock last night when I laid behind her. How soft and silky her skin was where my hand lay all night.

I pumped my cock harder and faster as my arousal spiked. She looked so fucking sexy all day yesterday with only my shirt on; it was like having my own pin-up-era porn star walking around my house, teasing me. Her tits were large and perky, leaving nothing to the imagination, they swayed heavily with each of her movements and they all but begged me to hold them in my hands for her.

I still had the images of them burned into my memory from when I had changed her, and my mouth watered as I thought about how perfect her hard nipples were. I could feel my teeth ache, longing to feel the flesh between them.

So I'd stood there in my shower and stroked my cock until I exploded with one of the most powerful orgasms I'd ever had as she laid upstairs, willing and wanting.

And clearly, I was a fucking idiot. Which was why I was still downstairs and she was in my bed, alone.

Standing in the dark living room, I knew Dev was going to stay up with her all night, betraying me. I made my way to the liquor cabinet for a nightcap, hoping it would help me drift off to sleep.

When I went for the whiskey though, it was gone, and so was the glass I'd planned on using.

I turned and looked up at the railing to the loft to see if I could see or hear anything from her, but it was silent.

There was no way she was sleeping, not after taking my best whiskey and dog upstairs, leaving me thirsty and lonely.

Fuck, my life was what country songs fucking *thrived* on.

So I grabbed another bottle and forcefully closed the cupboard, hoping she knew I was angry, and went to the couch.

I didn't even bother with the glass and drank straight from the bottle, and after about twenty minutes I felt the familiar warmth that the alcohol left fall over my body, numbing everything around the edges.

I looked up from the couch to the loft once more, hoping to glimpse her, but she never came to the edge for me, no matter how hard I tried beckoning her with my mind.

The house was dead silent and my drunk mind was finally relaxed when a sound drifted over the edge of the loft to me. It was so soft, at first I thought I'd imagined it. I leaned forward, trying to focus on what it was, trying to get the alcohol to clear for me to pinpoint it.

And then I figured out what it was, and a wave of regret washed over me, wishing I could turn back time by thirty seconds and warn myself not to listen.

She had just figured out what kind of asshole I really was, and that realization made me feel like the biggest one in the world.

The noise was that of her cries, muffled in the pillow, followed by Dev's sympathetic whine.

I remained on the couch, listening to her cries for the next two hours until she fell silent. I forced myself to do so, needing to hear them, to feel like the piece of trash I was, so that I wouldn't be tempted to give her any affection again.

It wasn't fair to her; she didn't deserve my inability to want her without my guilt and shame tainting it.

She was the definition of perfection. I knew almost nothing about her, but I could tell she was perfect. She was gorgeous, easily the most beautiful woman I'd ever met before, even through the bruises, that was easy to see.

And more than that, she was kind.

She was the type of woman who wouldn't hurt a fly and was so soft-spoken that when she yelled at me earlier; it shocked me senseless. She was kind, soft, and pure, but she also had a fire in her soul. And that fire burned when I treated her poorly, and a part of me felt pride in my chest, knowing she didn't let anyone put her down or belittle her.

At least until whoever got his hands on her and beat her so badly, she ended up here with me. It still bothered me immensely that she wouldn't tell me what happened to her, but if I thought about it enough, I found I couldn't blame her.

It had to have been a random attack.

Perhaps a carjacking or something.

I imagined someone carjacked and kidnapped her, beat her, and then dumped her somewhere.

It had to be something random like that. No one local would have done that to her, of that I was positive.

But as I laid my head back against the cushions and stared at the railing to my bedroom, I couldn't shake the feeling that what happened wasn't over for her just yet. And that made me angry because she had been through enough. If there was any way for me to stop more harm from coming to her, I had to try. But I had to get her to open up to me to do that.

My body was antsy and jumpy even after the copious amounts of booze I'd forced down my throat. My hands itched to feel her skin against them again. I leaned forward, resting my elbows on my knees as I tried to remind myself of all the reasons to stay away from her. But soon, I lost the battle and without even thinking about it; I stood up and my feet led me to the stairs.

I climbed the stairs, telling myself the entire way that I'd just check on her and make sure she was alright, then return to the couch. When I looked around the corner of the bedroom wall, I could make out the shape of her curled under the covers from the glow of the fire downstairs.

Her tiny female shape was tucked in deep, surrounded by blankets and pillows in my bed.

In my room.

In my home.

It stirred a sense of possessiveness inside of me, waking up the protector inside of me that I'd let go dormant for so long.

Too long.

She needed me. There was no refuting that, neither of us could deny that, so there was no point in trying anymore.

I had no intention of trying to stay away from her any longer. I had to trust my instincts, as I had always done before someone stole my life, leading to self-doubt.

Because my gut told me that from the very first scream I heard of hers, she was mine.

She needed me.

Before I could talk myself out of it and make any more excuses why I shouldn't let myself follow what my body so badly wanted, I ripped my shirt off over my head and shoved my pants down to my feet before kicking them across the room.

Dev lay on the bed behind the tiny woman and raised his head curiously at me as I stripped. I didn't doubt in my head that if he thought I was some threat to her, he would have torn me to shreds at my first move. Instead, he got up gently and jumped off the bed before clamoring down the stairs to the living room where he usually slept.

As I turned back towards the bed, I caught her looking over her shoulder at me, anger flooded from her red swollen eyes before she rolled back over to face the opposite wall in silent defiance.

I pulled the blanket back on my side and slid under it before pressing flush to her back, bending my legs into the bend of hers.

She gasped slightly when I slid my hand up her leg from knee to hip, feeling her bare skin until my fingers brushed the hem of her shirt bunched around her waist.

"Shh." I cooed from behind her as I buried my nose in the hair at her neck, before nudging it aside to bare her ear. She smelled so damn good, even with the musk of my soap on her skin. I nuzzled my cheek against the soft shell of her ear and neck and felt her shiver from head to toe as my beard stimulated the sensitive skin.

"Kip." She sighed softly.

"I just want to sleep in my bed, Hadley," I said as I slid my hand up over her hip, feeling it bare of any fabric where I should have felt the band of a pair of panties. I growled deep in my chest at the sensation of her warm, soft skin. "And I want to feel your lush body pressed against mine while I do it."

She was panting in the dark as my fingers played with that sensitive spot between her navel and her hip bone.

She was as turned on as I was.

Her hips flexed as she ground her thighs together, trying to get comfortable. The motion rocked her luscious ass against my groin, rubbing it across my hardening cock beneath my briefs.

"Mmh, you feel so good against me, *Bambina*. You're so small in my arms, but you fill my hands perfectly."

She arched her back, pressing her ass into my cock harder before grinding her hips again as she softly moaned. She turned her face back over her shoulder towards me, and her eyes were on fire. They glowed fiery green, and I could feel the passion in her body by just looking at them.

I leaned down and kissed her neck before pulling the shirt to the side, licking along her shoulder and gently biting the flesh.

"Don't play with my head, Kip. Don't play with my body if you're just going to play with my head." Her voice was light like it usually was, but I could feel the iron in it at the same time.

"I'm done playing, Hadley, I'm done fighting this. I'll burn in hell for stealing your light with my darkness, but I'm going to dance in your sun for as long as you'll let me."

She didn't answer me with anything more than a shuddered breath as I ran my hand up her torso, gently so I didn't hurt her ribs, letting only my calloused fingertips glide across the supple skin of her stomach and then to the underside of her breast.

"Tell me to stop and I will. Just say stop and I'll stop, no questions asked. Got it?" I inquired, and she swiftly nodded while her hand smoothly slid down and under her shirt to meet mine, where it had come to a halt. "I need to hear the words Hadley; tell me you got it."

"I got it, Kip. I'll tell you when to stop." She whispered into the darkness around us. She then guided my hand up further until the weight of her breast filled my palm, leaving more spilling out around it. Her tiny hand was on the back of mine and as I ran my fingers over her hard nipple, her nails dug into the skin of my knuckles.

I pulled my fingers off completely and then brought them back around her nipple, teasing and pulling on it as it puckered even further under my touch.

"Mmh." She moaned sensually. Her hips jerked as I pulled the nipple with more pressure before letting go of it.

I shifted my arm, gliding it down from beneath her neck to settle on her waist, where my hand then connected with her stomach as my fingertips delicately brushed beneath her belly button.

Even though I had just jacked off in the shower a couple of hours ago, I was impossibly hard again. My cock nestled between her bare ass cheeks and my hips involuntarily thrust, grinding it between us. I pulled her tighter against me with my hand that was flat on her stomach as she rotated her hips seductively before bumping her ass up to slide up the length of me before sliding back down.

The shirt she was wearing, which I recognized as one of mine from my drawer, had ridden up until it pooled just below her breasts. With my hand toying with her nipple, I lifted the shirt until she caught on and helped me slide it up and off of her completely. With her skin completely exposed, I gently pulled her shoulder back and leaned towards her, ensuring her hips remained on her side while her alluring movements continued in my lap. However, she angled her upper body towards me, allowing me to fully appreciate the enticing view.

"You are hands down the most beautiful woman I've ever seen before." Dropping my lips to hers, capturing them in a savage, erotic kiss. I used my hand on the opposite side of her face to pull her back towards me ever further as I licked and sucked her lips while the hand at her waist inched lower.

I knew the second my fingertips felt the wet heat of her pussy I'd be lost to her forever, I'd never be the same and I'd never be able to walk away, but that was exactly what I wanted the most.

I wanted something to tie me to her, something to claim her as mine.

So I leaned down and took her nipple between my lips, sucking it hard before biting it, causing her to arch her back, pushing it deeper into my mouth as I slid my fingers the last inch and into the slick heaven of her pussy.

And for the first time in years, I felt like I was where I belonged.

Chapter 7- Hadley

Molly

Jesus.

Fucking.

Hell.

As his lips indulged at my breast, my back arched in a painful yet pleasurable way, the gentle nip of his teeth adding a hint of delightful pain to my puckered nipple. However, I found myself capable of enduring it all without being overwhelmed.

I actually wanted more.

His hand slid lower and buried his fingers in my wetness as he rubbed the calluses of his hands over my hypersensitive clit.

"Fucking hell, you're so wet, Hadley. So fucking hot and perfect." He growled against my breast.

I was still on my side, with my torso turned toward him as he explored my pussy.

It felt so fucking good, my hips jerked and bucked under his hand as my ass ground deeper onto his cock between me and his stomach.

He was fucking big. Seriously huge and I thirsted to feel him inside of me.

It would hurt, but I craved the pain I knew he'd bring me.

His pain was so different from the pain the *Saint* had inflicted. I reveled in Kip's pain. I danced in the burn and moaned at the torment.

And I was fucking crazy.

But I couldn't worry about that right now, I wanted his crazy more than my next breath.

As he slid two fingers over my clit, I humped his cock. He was teasing my entrance with the tips of his fingers as I bucked and rode his hand, his tongue never leaving my breasts.

Kip played me like a fiddle for a while, rimming the entrance of my pussy where I so desperately needed him and then moving up to pinch and pull at my clit before grinding his big fingers against it in circles. He brought me so close to an orgasm over and over but held off.

"Please, Kip." I moaned pathetically as I reached behind me and palmed his cock, sliding my nails over it through the fabric of his briefs from balls to tip.

"Say it, Hadley. Beg me for it." He kissed his way up to my neck, where he bit down gently before soothing the pain with his tongue, then moving on and leaving another mark over the marks that were already there from before. He was claiming me over them.

"Make me come, please. Please let me come." I whined and rejoiced when I felt his smile against the skin right below my ear.

"You're such a good girl, so perfect. So perfectly mine." And with that, he buried two thick fingers deep inside of me, eliciting a gasp and shudder from my lips as I turned back onto my side completely to ride his expert fingers.

His praise was a drug, the absolute best I'd ever tasted. I needed the affirmation more than I needed anything else before in my life. I longed for it.

I kept my hand on his cock, his hips kept thrusting it between my ass cheeks. I could tell he was close too, and I knew he wanted his release, but I didn't know if I could handle actual sex with him. He didn't give me a long time to worry about it before his fingers curled inside of me, rubbing deliciously on the bundle of nerves inside of me that shot red-hot lightning through my limbs and spine.

"Fuck!" I gasped as the orgasm that had been building exploded inside of me. I convulsed in his arms as he held onto me, never letting up on my pussy or my sensitive nipples.

I felt his cock tense up even more in my hand and heard him grunt as warmth pooled inside of his briefs as he came in my hand. We both rode out the waves of ecstasy at each other's hands and then laid there, trying desperately to catch our breaths.

My skin was slick with sweat, and I let go of his glorious cock to whip the blankets off of me, welcoming the cool air.

He slowly withdrew his fingers from my clenched pussy before drawing lazy circles over my clit as he finally took his hands from me completely.

With a captivating gaze, he raised his fingers to his mouth and sensually licked them clean, as if relishing the taste.

I nearly exploded all over again. Normally, such a brazen act would repulse me and send me running, but watching him taste me intimately felt like he was claiming them as his in an incredibly powerful way. His stare never left mine as I watched him feast on his fingers.

"You taste like honey. It's incredibly arousing, and my new favorite flavor."

I just laid there silently, watching him over my shoulder, unable to form words. The alcohol I drank earlier had blurred the edges of my inhibitions, and when I felt his hard, desirable body behind mine when he got into bed, I couldn't bring myself to tell him to go away. I just wanted to feel secure and sexy, and that was how he made me feel every time he was near, when lust filled his eyes instead of the anger that usually was there.

He leaned forward and kissed me tenderly on the lips, lingering and tasting the seam of them before pushing through with his tongue to dance with mine. I'd never kissed a man with a beard before but as he deepened the kiss, I brought my hand up to his cheek and ran my nails through it, which he answered with a growl before rolling me over on my back and really putting all he had into it.

I laid on my back and opened my arms and my legs to him unconsciously, but he held back. He kissed me deeply but didn't move to lie between my legs like I wanted him to.

He slowly pulled back from the kiss and just looked down at me, almost in wonderment before he allowed his eyes to trail down my body, taking in my entire naked form laying in his bed. I moved to cover my breasts with my arms and pressed my legs together tightly.

"Don't." He commanded, his eyes snapping back up to mine. "Don't cover yourself and keep all of your beauty from me. I still can taste your orgasm on my tongue Hadley, you have nothing to hide from me any-more."

But I couldn't convince my arms to drop to my sides, even with the darkness working as a type of cover.

He scowled down at me, putting his features back into what I recognized most about him, and rolled over and got out of bed.

Did that piss him off?

I quickly dropped my hands, as much as it physically pained me to leave myself so vulnerable.

While he stood up, he kept his back to me; however, as he took a step towards the door, he glanced back at me over his shoulder and abruptly halted upon seeing me lying there completely exposed and vulnerable.

When he turned around, his gaze consumed me, mapping out a path over my skin that felt like a tangible caress. I lay there, striving to remain perfectly still.

He stepped back to the bed and knelt down, leaning over my face.

"Thank you," he murmured softly before giving me another gentle kiss. He stood again and turned towards the door once more, though. "I'm going to go clean myself up. This was the first time since I was a teenager that I've been so turned on that I came in my boxers. That's the effect you have on me."

I smiled in the darkness but once again remained silent as he went downstairs to the bathroom. I contemplated putting the shirt I'd stolen from his drawer back on, but somehow knew he wouldn't like that very much.

That I was doing or not doing something based on a man's reaction should have terrified me, or it should have at least enraged me. But I actually felt a sense of excitement and bravery.

Instead of putting the shirt back on, I drew the blankets back up over my body and laid back into the comfortable bed.

It wasn't long before he was climbing the stairs to the loft again, but I could feel my eyes drifting sleepily.

I didn't know what I was expecting to see as he crossed the threshold, but what I got was far more enjoyable than what I could probably have dreamed up.

He was as naked as the day he was born, holding a bitten apple and a stem of grapes. My eyes, of course, instantly went to the enormous package swinging proudly between his legs and then traveled over his body cut from stone. My eyes snapped back up to his face in embarrassment after staring at his cock and abs for so long.

He stopped and smirked at me mischievously, before taking another bite out of his apple and then dropping both arms to rest at his side. "Take a long look, baby. Soak it all in, I'm not shy."

I smiled embarrassingly and dropped my eyes to my hands on top of the blankets as I chewed on my lip. I couldn't possibly just stare at him like he said to. No way.

"I mean it, Hadley. Look at me, tell me what you like. Talk to me." He sounded calm and sincere, and I baited myself into looking back up at him, careful not to stray too long on my way up.

His joking face had faded slightly, and I could see the seriousness in his gaze once again. "What are you attracted to the most about my appearance?" He asked once more.

My eyes skimmed over the strong defined muscles of his shoulders, down his biceps, and lengthy arms with veins and muscle fibers straining under the swirls of ink. I cut my gaze back across his chiseled chest and lean abdomen.

I felt the heat slide up my chest and face as I allowed myself to look down at his cock again. He had a trim down there, but the black hair that sprinkled over his chest and stomach extended down further to his groin before thinning out over his thighs and calves once again.

"I like how masculine you are." My response was weak, so I swallowed quickly and sat up further, try-ing to make myself not seem so meek and pathetic. He waited patiently, standing naked as I continued to look him over. "I like how feminine your masculinity makes me feel. And how confident you are. How big you are," I paused as I looked down at his waist and raised one eyebrow before looking back up at him, "everywhere, and how strong you are."

His eyes lit up as he listened silently. He closed the distance between us and slid into the bed next to me, still saying nothing. I waited as patiently as I could, then started second-guessing my answers. What if he wanted only the superficial sexual answers, and I just went all deep and got my feelings all over him?

But he set the fruit down in his lap as he slid down under the blankets before wrapping his arm around me and pulling me in to lie on his chest with my head on his shoulder.

"Your femininity makes me feel strong and masculine. I've never been with a woman as small and delicate as you are, but I'm finding it to be like a drug for the alpha inside of me."

In a very un-lady-like way, I snorted and said, "I think alpha describes you perfectly." He plucked a grape from the bunch in his lap and pressed it into my lips. When I opened them and sucked it into my mouth, he grunted from under me, making me look up once more.

"Every single thing you do is erotic, Hadley. Literally every single thing." He finished the apple and put it in the bin next to the bed before popping a few grapes in his own mouth and then offering me another. "I mean it when I tell you that you're so incredibly beautiful, and I can see that you don't believe me, but I'll work on getting you to start some other day. Your eyes are an incredible color of green and they draw me in from across the room every single time I catch your gaze. I could spend an entire day just doing things to get you to look at me." He paused briefly, "And your body," he slid his hand down to graze over my curves before settling it on my hip with his big palm resting on my backside, "Your body makes me want to do crazy, beautifully, awful things to it. But more than just physically, your calm and quiet nature soothes me, too. It plays with the alpha in me and makes me want to just protect and listen to you for the rest of my days. And I don't know the last time I've felt that way so instantaneously before. I don't think I ever have."

"I won't ask what this means," I motioned between our bodies, "but I will ask if this means you're done treating me like a pariah?" My fingers played across his chest and abdomen, teasing the sensitive flesh there below the ink. He placed his hand over mine before lifting it to his lips, where he placed a gentle kiss on the inside of my wrist.

"I apologize for my attitude the last few days. It's been a very long time since I've had anyone here with me, and I only acted like that because I was trying to fight whatever this draw is between us. This," he paused, setting my hand back down on his stomach before threading his fingers through mine, "is very uncharted territory for me, okay? I don't know what it is or what it will be or where it's going from here, but just know that I'm interested in you for more than just sex. Okay?"

I lifted my head to look at him and could see, for the first time, the vulnerability in his eyes as he looked down at me and waited for me to answer. "I don't know what it is or what it will be or where it's going from here, either. But I'm interested in you for more than just sex, too. We can figure it out one day at a time."

I put a smile on my face and laid my head back down on his chest as he set the grapes on the end table and settled deeper into the bed. When he reached to turn the light off, though, I could decipher a few words from a script tattoo on the inside of his upper arm.

Molly, my one true love, my soulmate amongst imposters.

Chapter 8 - Kip

Good Enough

I prayed for hours that I wasn't making a mistake. I laid there with the perfect tiny angel that had fallen into a trap on my property, in my arms after I'd explored her body and found pleasure in it and prayed that I hadn't just betrayed the only woman I'd ever loved.

Hadley had laid awake for a long time in my arms too, I felt the variance in her breathing the same way I was sure she felt mine as we lay in silence and got lost in our own thoughts.

When she rolled away, to lie on her side facing the wall, I let her go and didn't follow her. I wanted to, but I needed to wrap my head around how effortlessly I consumed her body with mine earlier. How little thought and effort it took to convince myself to betray Molly and cheat on her with the tiny pixie.

Would she be mad if she knew? Or would she know I was a weak man who couldn't have said no to such an easy, willing partner when she was lying half naked in my bed?

Shit. Hadley wasn't fucking easy.

She was the opposite of easy and I knew that. Deep down, she had been struggling with her own inner demons the entire time she had been with me, but especially when I was touching her.

Did she have someone waiting for her at home that she had just betrayed like I had? Or did her reservations and worries stem from what someone did to her? She told me many times that she didn't have anyone, but how could she not?

She was beautiful, even more beautiful than Molly, and believe me, it pained me to admit that.

Molly had always been the girl next door type of pretty, with easy, low maintenance routines that left her effortlessly pretty. Tall and skinny, with long blond hair and crystal blue eyes. But Hadley was timeless and elegant in an Elizabeth Taylor way. A pin up, goddess type of sex appeal paired with a submissive and gentle personality that left my head spinning and my cock hard constantly.

I didn't deserve her affection. And I didn't deserve her kindness, seeing as how I'd barely given her any of my own since she showed up. But I wanted to change that.

I wanted to be nice to her and stop being such a hard ass with her, given that she surely didn't deserve it. But I couldn't let my grief and resentment go, it'd been five years, and I was still a pissed off shell of the man I'd been before two men stole everything I ever wanted and needed in my life.

And I didn't know how to just let someone else in when I'd shut down and shut out everyone I had left five years ago.

But I needed to figure it out because the snow stopped falling earlier, and by the day after next, the roads would be passable and I'd be out of excuses for keeping her locked away with me and not taking her into town like I'd told her I would.

She hadn't brought it up, and I sure didn't either, but she would eventually, and I'd then have to shut up and take her to town and give her what she needed to get away from me and back to her life. Or figure out how to convince her to stay here and see what it was becoming with me.

And I didn't know how to even begin wooing her into staying.

Scratch that.

I did know how to start, and that involved being kind, sweet, and gentle with her. Once upon a time, I was all of those things with Molly; I could figure it out with Hadley.

I looked over at her and admired the way her curves laid out under the blankets, her waist was so tiny and her hips wide with a flare that made me ache to hold them in my hands and pull her backward into me.

So I did what my body ached for me to do and rolled over, wrapping my arms around her from behind and holding her the entire night as I once again slept harder than I had in years.

When I woke up the next morning, she was still in bed, but she was awake, looking at me from where she laid on her side facing me.

"Mmh, good morning," I said as I scooted closer and pulled her warm naked body flush with mine. She giggled lightly when my morning erection jabbed into her stomach before it laid between us.

"Good morning to you, too." She whispered. Her dimples were so deep in her supple cheeks, I wanted to lean forward and just take a bite out of each of them.

"Your gorgeous face is something I could easily get used to waking up to every morning. I can't even tell you the last time I've slept past sunrise, but I've done it every morning since you got here."

She smiled, "I've never been an early riser before, but since getting here, I'm up with the sun. Must be all the wonderful windows."

"Must be, I'll have to get some curtains for you," I said.

Instead of acknowledging the way she stiffened in my arms slightly as I talked about the future, I buried my face in her neck and breathed her in. I kissed her neck with open passionate kisses and planned on pulling back after a little teasing, but she moaned sugary sweetness and dug her nails into my shoulders where she held on as I tasted her flesh.

I willingly accepted her invitation.

As I slid my knee forward and spread hers, she greeted me by throwing her leg up over my hip and opening her center to me, rocking forward on my thigh.

"Tell me what you want, *Bambina*." I whispered as I kissed up her neck to the shell of her ear, remembering how responsive she was to the stimulation last time. I ran my tongue along the outer edge before sucking the lower lobe into my mouth. She squirmed in my arms, rocking her hips on my thigh until I felt her wet center grind against my own naked flesh.

"Tell me what *Bambina* means." She replied, catching me off guard, but not really surprising me, as she had asked me before and I'd avoided the question.

I smiled at her persistence and pulled back to look into her eyes as I let my hand slide from her back to rest on her hip before slowly sliding it around to her front and teasing the upper outer lips of her pussy pressed against my leg. "Are you sure that's what you want right now?" I asked, once more trying to distract her.

"Yes." She said even as she moaned, closing her eyes, and arching her back to press harder on my fingers. "I want you to tell me what it means, and then I want you to lay me back and finally slide that monster cock deep into me until it bottoms out. Think you can do all that for me?"

Naughty little chit.

I felt the fire climb in my veins and blast to my cock as her words rushed through my ears. She opened her eyes and watched me intently, waiting for a reply.

"I think I can handle that." Swiftly flipping her onto her back, I positioned myself on top of her. I was careful not to put any pressure on her ribs or bad hand as I slid between her open legs. My cock pressed against her wet pussy as I slid it back and forth, teasing us both immensely.

"Kip." She moaned, running her nails down my pecs and stomach until she reached between us and slid her hand between my cock and my pelvis, and pressed me harder into her clit before stroking it eagerly. "Tell me what it means so you can take me, right here, right now."

I growled at her and threw my head back as the sensations made my balls ache with a need to bottom out in her like she'd told me to.

I dropped my head until our faces were inches apart and stopped moving, taking a few deep breaths to focus. When her eyes opened and looked back into mine, her hand stilled, and she waited for my reply. "It's Italian, for little girl." I said, watching her reaction. She stayed silent and still, other than the slight squinting of her eyes at the definition. She didn't like that answer, of that I was sure.

"My sweet, feisty bambina." I smoothed the hair back from her forehead and smiled down at her before leaning down to kiss her sweetly. She welcomed my lips on her own, even though she didn't like my answer. I made sure to remember that. "My grandfather has called my grandmother that their entire marriage. It's to remind her of how small and feminine she is in his big powerful arms, and how he feels like her protector when he is holding her."

"Oh." She whispered.

"The moment you opened your eyes here in my bed, I finally understood what he meant my entire life when he told me to find someone that needs me as much as I need them to," I said as I ground my hips into hers further. She ran her tongue out over her plump lower lip before biting down on it as her eyes closed in pleasure. "We have an indescribable connection, Hadley. And I'm going to shield you and protect you as long as you let me."

She seemed to hold her breath as she softly whispered, "And if you can't? If my demons aren't something you can physically protect or shield me from? Then what?"

I paused for a moment, absorbing her question and the fear in her eyes, "What are your demons?"

Her green eyes dilated slightly before her lids closed and when they opened again, they were looking at a spot just to the side of my face instead of back at me as they had been before.

"Tell me," I demanded, sliding my hips forward again, rubbing my cock through her soaked folds.

She scowled at me slightly before stretching her neck back and moaning slightly as I used the head of my cock to put pressure on the bundle of nerves at her core.

"I can't, you wouldn't want me anymore if I did." She whispered against my lips before sliding her fingers into the hair at the base of my neck, pulling me down the fraction of an inch left between us, and kissing me with lust-filled noises. "And I need you right now, so bad. I can't risk it." She finished as she wrapped her legs around my hips and pulled me against her even more.

And I was lost.

I buried my fingers in her dark locks and kissed her hard as I pulled my hips back far enough for the crown of my cock to find her slick opening and surged forward, spearing her fully in one thrust.

She let out a screech as her tight pussy fought to accommodate my size, but I didn't stop as I pulled back and thrust forward again as my eyes rolled in the back of my head.

"Fuck Hadley, you feel so damn good," I growled, already feeling the electric current at the base of my spine pick up.

"You're so big, you fill me up like no other." She moaned.

I leaned down and took one of her perfect nipples in my mouth, flicking it with my tongue before biting down on it, making her yell out in ecstasy again.

"Yes! I'm so close already, Kip." She ran her fingernails up my flanks and up to my shoulders before running them back down again, driving me wild.

I pounded into her repeatedly, pushing her up the bed further with each brutal thrust. Her eyes closed again, and she threw her head back as her body clamped down on my cock as she orgasmed. It was an entire-body experience, and I watched with rapture as it overtook her.

The sight of her losing it caused me to pitch over the top and climax myself. I filled her with everything I had and ached to do it again and again in an animalistic way. I didn't know her from Adam, but I wanted to fucking claim her in the most fundamental way. A way I had once before with Molly. It was something I lost the day I lost her.

Taking a moment to catch my breath and calm down, I carefully pulled out and rolled onto my back, bringing her along and holding her securely against my chest with both arms.

"I didn't use a condom; I should have asked you if it was alright before I just took you like that." I panted.

For the first time in my life, the pleasure overtook me and made me not care about safety.

"I have a birth control implant in my arm, so that's all good. And I've never had sex without a condom." There was a darkness shadowing her eyes as she said it though.

"Okay, we're good then." I exhaled with relief.

"Very good." She said, taking a deep breath and relaxing into my arms. I looked down at her and saw her smile as she tried to hide it in my chest, bashfully.

"Oh yeah? How good?" I questioned, though I already knew the answer, for myself at least.

"Eh, just good." She tried to play it off, but I used my hands to tickle her arms as she lied, and she ended in a fit of girlish giggles and I had never heard a more angelic sound in my life.

Laughing myself, I pulled her over the top of me and spread her thighs over mine as I laughed with her, but she quickly sobered up.

"Was it good for you? Was I good?" She asked shyly, not meeting my eyes.

I slid my fingers under her chin and made her look at me square on before I answered. I could tell she needed my answer to be a good one to ease some fear or doubt buried deep in her heart.

"Honestly, what we just did and what we did last night felt better than anything I've ever felt before, with anyone. Better than anything I could ever imagine."

I saw the speculation in her eyes as she tried to cover it up, but she wasn't quick enough. So instead, I showed her, so she would have to believe me.

I grasped her hips with both hands and urged her towards me until my hardened cock entered her again.

I spent the rest of the day inside of her, showing her in ways she couldn't deny, just how *good* it was for me.

Chapter 9 - Hadley

I had fallen out of a nightmare and into a dream come true. I awoke most mornings with a sense of wonderment and girl-like happiness that only the quiet, sleep-filled space could conjure. But it was always short-lived because when realization dawned on where I was, memories also flooded my brain of where I had come from before. How did I live in the present when the past was still so near and to blame for bringing me here?

I never laid there too long thinking of the past though, because Kip was quick to rise once he sensed I had woken, and he was quicker to consume my body with his. His sexual appetite was insatiable, and he was often bringing me to orgasm before, after, and sometimes during his workday. I couldn't complain, but when I was alone in the silence, my brain couldn't help but wonder how I could be so okay with letting Kip in physically after all I had been through.

We hadn't connected emotionally as well as we had physically, and that was on both of us. We each had big scary demons in our closet that threatened to upheave the peaceful dynamic we had fallen into, but we didn't know the extent of each other's darkness.

He never spoke of his past further back than a few years. Not a word, not a slip-up, not a snippet of who he was before at all. It was as though he didn't exist a few years ago. He spoke of a few friends he had from town and a few interactions he had with them, but they sounded superficial and not like he had a deep connection with them.

The snow had stopped a few days ago; I knew the roads were being cleared, though we still had heard no plows or traffic, but I didn't know if I ever would, as I still hadn't seen the road from the cabin. My free time was quickly ending, and I wasn't ready to give it up just yet. I craved Kip's touch and the snippets of himself he let me see from time to time like I craved the heat within his home and bed.

The sun was falling out of the sky quickly as evening approached, and Kip and Dev would be returning soon.

It was my favorite time of day. I had dinner cooked and kept warm in the oven when he walked in, shaking the cold off of him as he did. When his eyes found me sitting in his armchair with a book in my lap, a small, satisfied smile graced his face.

"That chair looks good on you."

I smiled at the sentiment and slowly stood up, "Dinner is ready and waiting for you if you want to eat now or shower first."

"You cooked?" He asked, surprised. I hadn't made anything since breakfast a few days ago. He had everything prepped and ready to go in the morning each day, so I hadn't felt comfortable stepping in, but today I took the lead.

"I did, I hope you like vegan vegetable soup with a side of tofu." I worked hard

maintaining my composure, but when I got a look at the disbelief that crossed his face as he listened, I quickly lost the battle and smiled, giving myself away.

Relief crossed his face a second before a mischievous look took its place. "I knew I didn't have any of that crap, but you almost got me."

"I sure tried." Stepping forward, he smiled back at me and softly wrapped his hands around my waist, drawing me into his chest. "I made baked ziti and garlic bread. Simple but filling. And for dessert, I made chocolate pudding using a box I found in your cupboard, so I can't be held responsible for the taste."

"It all sounds almost as good as you do." He said as he leaned down into my neck and inhaled as he held me. He loved having his face buried there with his lips on the sensitive skin.

"Mmh" was all I could manage as I held onto him.

"Shower with me. I'll wash your back and you can wash mine." He said.

It didn't bother me he didn't ask me to; I knew if I had protested, he would have let me. But there wasn't a single reason on this earth to keep me out of his shower with him, so I nodded my acceptance as he picked me up under my thighs and carried me into the spacious bathroom. He set me on the counter as he stepped back, stripped off his shirts, and unbuckled his belt and jeans before stepping over to the stone shower, turning it on and letting it warm up.

I sat on my perch and enjoyed the show as he moved around, getting towels and toiletries ready. His body was so muscular and toned, watching them ripple under the black and grey ink on his skin was sinful and

I couldn't look away. When he reached back into the shower to check the temperature, I read a bit of script along his ribs on the left side of his chest.

Improvise, adapt, and overcome.

He turned back around quickly, and I tried to hide that I was looking at the words. I didn't know why I felt like a voyeur when deciphering his tattoos, but it felt personal, and I didn't feel like we were on a personal level. Although he had been inside of my body multiple times, matters of the heart and head were very different.

"Are you okay?" He asked as he walked back over to me.

A serious look in his eyes told me I was reacting to the tattoo more than I wanted to be. I couldn't be sure, but I thought that saying was military.

Another snippet into the life of Kip. Was he military? Past or present? He fit the look of a soldier in most ways. Strong, stern, and serious.

He most definitely had some military background.

"Yeah, I'm good," I replied, letting the tension roll out of my shoulders as I smiled back up at him.

"Good, because the water is perfect and so are you, so I need to get you naked and in the shower before I embarrass myself here on the tile floor."

With a devilish chuckle, he assisted me in removing my shirt and unclasping my bra. I watched his eyes as he did, feeling them cascade down my chest to my breasts. I could feel his gaze as I watched him. It was nearly as pleasurable as his physical touch. "Embarrass yourself like you did in your boxers the first time you made me come?" I asked as I leaned forward, pressing my hard nipples to the coarse hair on his chest.

"Hilarious. I can't help how attracted I am to you." He said as he reached up and allowed the back of his fingers to trace down from my collarbones to my aching nipples.

Once again, I couldn't speak, so I resorted to moaning and leaning into his touch.

He dropped his pants and lifted me to slide mine down my legs, leaving us both naked and panting before he lifted me again and carried me into the shower.

He was gentle and caring as he slid into my still healing body. I gasped as I struggled to take his girth and size, but soon I was riding him back with just as much vigor and passion as my body accommodated him. He knew my body so well already; he had me on the edge of a climax soon and then tipping over the edge into ecstasy, following soon after.

We stood in the hot steam of the water, in sated silence, as he washed my hair. His talented fingers scrubbed my scalp and down my neck, easing tense muscles.

"Hmm." I hummed and let my body lean back into his. "You could trick me into thinking you knew what you were doing back there."

He hummed back and chuckled, "Maybe a time or two before."

That choice of words made me still as questions rose in my brain for the millionth time in the last week. "Have you been in a long-term relationship before?" My voice was steady but soft as I asked, braver with my back facing him, so he couldn't see the fear on my face.

I guess part of me was afraid of him admitting he was in one with someone else presently, while another part of me was afraid he would dodge the question all together.

"Have you?" He asked, choosing the second option.

I tried not to let disappointment at his avoidance show, as I turned and rinsed my hair under the water, pulling his fingers from the tresses reluctantly.

When my head was tipped back, I opened my eyes and caught sight of the scowl between his eyes at my abrupt turn. I closed my eyes again to shut it out.

"No." I stated truthfully, "I've never been seriously committed to anyone."

"How is that possible?" He asked, stepping forward and dropping his forehead to mine, wrapping his large hands around the widest part of my hips, and pulling my chest to his stomach, letting the water cascade over both of our faces.

With a shrug, I let my fingertips explore the hard planes of his abs and sides as if I were blind, reading a braille story. "I've never found anyone worthy of something serious. I moved around a lot and kept to myself most of the time."

He pulled back and looked down at me questioningly like he was trying to answer other questions with the answer I'd just given him.

Yeah, well, that's a two-way street bucko.

"When was your last serious relationship?" I asked. Figuring his lack of answer last time was an affirmation that he'd been in one before.

His eyes darkened noticeably, and he let his hands fall from my hips as he grabbed the shampoo and started washing his own hair.

I put my hand on his arm, "I was going to do that for you, to repay the favor." I smiled up at him, trying the adage you get more with sugar than spice.

"You can't reach it, so I'll get it."

His voice was gruff and his movements were sharp as he lathered up his hair with his eyes closed. He worked it into his beard and continued to stay silent and closed off as I stupidly stood there watching as his walls grew around his heart like an impenetrable force keeping us apart.

How were we ever going to get past the emotional barriers if neither of us were willing to go first?

My heart ached as the weight of my secrets weighed down on my soul once again.

I wrung my hair out and stepped out of the stone shower quietly. As I stood on the mat on the floor in the bathroom, I grabbed a towel and quickly wrapped it around my body.

"Hey." He said, popping his head into the entrance of the shower and looking for me. But I just walked out of the bathroom and went upstairs to find my clothes and put some sort of armor on over my naked body. "Hadley!" He called after me, but I ignored him.

The same way he ignored me when I was standing directly in front of him.

I was standing in the bedroom in a bra and panties when he walked up the stairs and stood silently, brooding with a towel around his waist and his fists on his hips.

"Why did you leave?" He asked.

"You were ignoring me. If you insist on shutting me out, I'm going to leave." I said as I grabbed a shirt to pull on. He reached forward quickly and grabbed it from my hands and threw it over the railing to the living room. "What the hell?" I snapped, turning on him.

"I wasn't ignoring you." He replied sharply.

"Bullshit." I retorted. "You weren't answering any of my questions, either."

His chest heaved dramatically as he looked down at me with his eyebrows knitted in the center, frustration radiated off his body. "So you just take off when you don't get your way?"

"This isn't about me getting my way, Kip! It's about you, unwilling to share anything about your past, yet expecting me to share about mine!"

"You aren't exactly an open book either, Hadley." He huffed.

I didn't bother to reply. We weren't going to resolve anything at the moment. I might be twelve years younger than him, but I could tell in terms of emotional maturity, we were both fucking lacking.

I looked in my bag for another shirt, but the one he chucked had been my last clean one.

Shit.

Making my way to his dresser, I opened the drawer where he usually kept his things and reached for one from the top. Just as I was about to grab it, he abruptly closed it, nearly trapping my fingers inside. I turned on him, "You threw mine! I need clothes!"

"The fuck you do." He said as he closed the distance between us and wound his fingers into my hair, pulling my head back to look up at him seconds before his lips crashed down on mine.

The wounds to my lips had healed, and I welcomed the bite of his mouth pressed roughly to them for the first time, every other kiss had been softer than what he was giving to me finally. He was vibrating with tension, and I knew if I gave in to him, he would be anything but gentle with me.

"You're crazy!" I growled out against his lips before sucking his bottom lip into my mouth and biting on it. His hands dropped from my hair and landed on my hips, turning us until my back pressed into the tall dresser.

"You make me fucking crazy." He spoke against my neck as his teeth sunk into my skin and bit.

"Oh, my god." I threw my head back into the wood of the drawers and dug my nails into his pecks as he sucked on the skin and licked it. "More," I begged, letting my fingers drop to the towel at his waist and ripping it open, baring him to my hungry eyes.

"You can run all you want, Hadley, but you can't hide from me." He said and then dropped to his knees in front of me and looked up at me. Even on his knees, his head came up to my breasts, and he wasted no time reaching around me to undo my bra and free my breasts to his waiting mouth and hands.

He sucked my nipple into his mouth and flicked it with his tongue as his hands grabbed both of my breasts and pressed them together. "I fucking love your tits." He groaned, switching to the other nipple as his fingers pinched the one his lips just left.

I threaded my fingers through his hair, pulled his head off my breasts, and leaned down and kissed him.

It wasn't a pretty kiss; it was feverish and all lips and teeth and passion and consumption.

He consumed me within himself as he drank from my lips and devoured my body with his hands.

He knelt down and positioned my leg over his shoulder, pulling my panties aside and burying his face between my thighs.

"Oh, my god!" I moaned, grabbing onto his hair, and riding his face as he fervently licked me.

"I'm far from heavenly, darling, but I'll make you think I am either way." He laughed into my flesh as he buried two fingers deep.

"Yes." I purred and grabbed onto the drawers behind me for support as he fucked me wildly with his fingers and tongue.

It took absolutely no time at all, and soon I was exploding into a technicolor orgasm as I rode his face madly.

He hardly waited for me to come down from the high before he stood up, shoved my panties down my legs, and walked me backward towards the bed. He laid me down and climbed up my body, lining himself up with my entrance and pushing in without warning.

"Oof." I groaned and widened my legs to accommodate him better.

"You have the tightest pussy I've ever buried myself in. Ever."

"Good. Something to keep you coming back for more." I played. I was on the dangerous side of needy in that moment and knew he could reject me, but I was hoping he would prove me wrong since our relationship had turned sometime in the previous days. We'd gone from killing time to enjoying it.

"As if." He said, leaning down into my neck and biting the skin of my shoulder softly, "I'm hooked on you, Hadley. I couldn't walk away now if I wanted to." He thrust in and out of my body, wildly drawing moans from my lips. "And believe me, I have no plans to walk away or let you walk away anytime soon, either."

I tried to keep my focus on his words as he said everything I was hoping for from him. I needed him desperately.

"Good." I moaned and then gasped as my orgasm ripped from my body, washing over me like a tidal wave of pleasure and pain as his thrusts became punishing. He fucked me straight into the mattress with such vigor and no remorse as I begged and pleaded for more.

I always needed more from the man.

"Mine." He growled as he chased his own pleasure. "You. Are. Mine. Hadley."

"Yes." I purred. "Fuck me like this every time, and I'll never even notice you hold me captive in a world of secrets and lies."

He growled in frustration as he pinned my legs over his forearms and rolled his hips, rubbing his pelvis against my clit. "You act as though you have no secrets or lies, Hadley. Like you're so different from me."

"I know," I answered truthfully. "But at least I don't pretend to be something I'm not." I clawed his arms with my nails as I hung onto him, challenging the beast inside of him. I don't know what came over me and made me test him like that. He could snap me like a twig if he wanted to, and looking deep into his dark eyes, he looked like he was considering doing just that. But I needed to say my peace about our dynamic.

He grunted and pulled out of my body and quickly rolled me over into doggy and slammed his cock back inside of me. "God, your ass is incredible." He hissed, filling both of his large hands with my flesh as he pounded me into the mattress.

I placed one palm flat against the wall over the bed and pushed back into his powerful thrusts, moaning and chasing my pleasure. I slid my other hand under my body and rubbed my clit, chasing my next orgasm.

"No." He said, pulling my hand away and slapping it to the wall next to my other one. "Your pleasure is mine. If you want to come, I'll be the one to make you." He growled, laying his body against my back and pumping his hips faster into me. His teeth bit and teased my ear as he slid his thick fingers down against my clit and rubbed perfectly, pushing me headfirst toward yet another powerful orgasm. "Good girl." He bit out in my ear when I moaned loudly. "You're so perfect for me."

"Don't stop!" I begged. "I need you." What I despised was how I had stopped antagonizing him and started begging him, but that's exactly what he did to me. He made me needy, but at least in that moment, he delivered.

"I'm right here, *bambina*. Come for me. I want to feel your body milking my come deep inside of you."

"Yes!" I cried, throwing my hips back into his and exploding in his arms. He held me tight, keeping me from falling face first into the bed as I lost my hold on the wall.

"Good girl." He praised into my ear. His hips were jerking madly, showing his impending orgasm, and moments later he bit my shoulder as he filled me up with his come, branding my insides and skin with his claim. "That's my pussy, baby. I'm never giving it up."

He moaned on and on, slowly thrusting his hips as his hands roved over my body as we caught our breaths. He let go of my shoulder and my body, gently laying me down on the bed and pulling out before collapsing next to me on the mattress. I laid limp on my stomach as he threw his arm over his eyes and relaxed.

"Holy shit, that was... holy shit." He said after a few minutes, and I smiled into the blankets.

"You should write hallmark cards." I joked, and he cracked one eye open and side eyed me.

"Funny girl." He deadpanned.

"I've been told that a time or two before." I laughed and scooted over to his side, and he pulled me against him until my head was on his chest. Silence descended on us and the weight of our argument before the sex started crushing the mood. Kip felt it too as he stared at the ceiling in the quickly darkening room.

"We should go eat." He said after a while, and I fought to contain the sigh that wanted to escape. Just like that, we were back to square one. Our bodies were so in sync that I could almost pretend he was a stranger to me.

Almost.

Instead of giving into my desire to scream for answers, I untangled my body from his and silently dressed in a flannel of his and a pair of sweatpants from my bag as he watched me from the bed in stillness.

I said nothing to him as I walked down the stairs and started arranging food on plates to serve. By the time he came down, I wasn't hungry as the questions and frustration knotted my stomach up and left me aching for anything from him he was willing to give me.

He sat down across from me and eyed my empty plate as he looked at his own heaping pile. "Why aren't you eating?" He asked, placing his hands next to his silverware as he watched me.

"Not hungry right the moment," I answered, taking a sip of the coffee I'd made with a splash of whiskey in it to ease my chaotic mind.

"You need to eat Hadley; your body needs the nutrients to heal itself," Kip said, and his voice lacked the authority or dominance it usually had when he gave me an instruction like that, and instead he was calm and tender.

"Answer a question and I'll take a bite," I replied quickly before I could think better of it.

His eyebrows rose, and he eyed my coffee cup that I clutched in both hands, on top of my knee. I was hugging it to my chest across from him, but he was on to me. He reached forward, took it from me, and sniffed. "Whiskey, huh?"

"Warms the soul. Or something like that." I said, devoid of any emotion.

"And loosens the tongue." He volleyed back.

"Then I'll answer one back for each one you answer."

He eyed me, considering it. "You'll answer any question I ask, without fail, and you'll eat a bite."

"I won't tell you who did this to me." I said quickly, "But I'll answer anything else."

He paused, looking down at my cup and then handing it back to me, probably figuring he'd get more out of me the lower my inhibitions were. "Deal."

He motioned for me to start with a question as he took a bite of his meal.

In the past few days, I had imagined all the questions I would ask him if given the opportunity. However, now that he was finally willing to answer them, I hesitated to ask the difficult ones because I wasn't sure if I was prepared for the challenging answers that would come with them.

"How long have you lived up here? Like this?" I asked and his chewing stopped, probably surprised by my direction.

"Four years." He said and then scooped up a big bite of ziti off his plate and held his fork out for me to eat. Leaning forward, I wrapped my lips around his fork and took a bite of food. Throughout the entire process, I kept my eyes locked on his, causing his pupils to dilate as he observed my chewing. "It's fucking good, isn't it?" He asked, fixated on my mouth.

"Mouthwatering," I answered back and his eyes snapped up from my lips to my eyes as he groaned.

"Where do you live?" He asked.

I finished chewing and took a sip of my coffee. "New York City was where I lived before coming here, but I was on my way to Florida when I got... sidetracked."

"Sidetracked." He repeated and then took another bite, not offering anything else.

"Why do you live out here alone like this?" I asked, watching him as he considered his answer.

"Because I like a hard days work to keep my body and mind from running wild."

I contemplated that as he reached forward with a piece of garlic bread and I took a bite, savoring the buttery garlic flavor as it exploded on my tongue.

God, I was an excellent cook.

"Why were you going to Florida?" He asked.

"Fresh start I guess. I was lonely in New York and believe it or not, I hate the cold."

He smirked at me and then shook his head. "Hell of a place to end up here, then."

"You're telling me," I said with a small smile of my own. I washed down the bread with my spiked coffee and then set down my cup, ready to ask some of the harder questions. "Are you married?"

His entire body went rigid as he watched me. "Why would you ask me that?"

I shook my head, standing firm in my position. "Answer me first." His rigid body was screaming at me to end this game, to protect myself from the pain I knew it would cause me, but I couldn't live here anymore without some further knowledge about him.

"I- I can't." He said, dropping my gaze and fisting his hands at the side of his plate.

"Why?" I felt my eyebrows drop over my eyes as fear coursed through my body.

"Because it will hurt you." He replied, looking up at me under his dark lashes quickly before dropping my gaze once again.

"How?" I shook softly in my chair, unable to come up with a single answer to that question that didn't threatened to destroy us before we even had a real chance to begin with. My chest ached, and my stomach rolled, my skin prickled, and my eyes burned as I sat there watching him as the silence stretched on.

"I can't." He repeated, shaking his head. "I can't cause you pain Hadley, don't ask that of me. Please." He whispered.

"This hurts me," I said, waving my hand back and forth between us. "Falling for a man that may be unavailable in more than one way Kip, that hurts. Not knowing if I'm the other woman here hurts. Reading her name on your body when you're doing such sweet and tender things to me." I gasped. "That hurts." My voice broke as tears pooled in my eyes.

His own eyes misted up as he looked at me, I was ripping open my heart and laying it on the floor at his feet and he was still silent.

"I can't." He said again, and I closed my eyes, feeling the tears crest over the lashes and running down my cheeks.

"Then I guess this is over," I said, leaving out exactly what I meant by *this*. I took my still-empty plate over to the cupboard and put it away, standing at the sink and looking out over the eerie snow-covered forest outside his home. "I think it's time I get a ride into town." Tears continued to fall down my cheeks.

Happiness had been so close; I had tasted it. I had felt it caress my skin and warm my heart from the inside out.

But all I felt now was cold.

Icy coldness gripped my soul and shattered my already broken heart.

I had been so close.

Chapter 10 – Kip

She stood at the sink in silence after telling me she wanted to get away from me and go back to her life. Pain erupted in my chest where my heart used to beat as I imagined taking her away from my home and watching her walk away from me for good.

I should do it.

She deserved to be rid of me.

But fuck, I couldn't make my body do what my brain told me to do. I couldn't let her leave me like this.

I stood up and carried my uneaten dinner to Dev's bowl and pushed it into the stainless steel. It was a fucking shame to do it too, because Hadley was an incredible cook and the ziti and garlic bread were the best I'd ever tasted before, but my appetite shriveled up with my heart when she asked about my wife.

God, hearing the word wife on the lips of the woman I was enamored with, gutted me.

Pain radiated through my chest as I turned to look at her back, but she wouldn't face me where she stood with her fingers gripping the edge of the sink in a death grip. "I'm going to go out and do some more chores. Keep Dev inside and lock the door behind me." I said, but she still didn't respond. I layered up and told Dev to stay when he tried to follow me out, and I walked out into the freezing night.

Letting out a heavy sigh under the cover of the porch, I slung the rifle over my back and watched as my breath evaporated into a mist above my head as the cold destroyed it.

The cold never bothered me before. But since feeling the warmth in Hadley's arms, I was aching for something more.

Something deeper than just the drifts under my feet as I walked down to the wood shack, intent on splitting logs for the fireplace until I couldn't lift my arms again.

Maybe after that, I could come up with a way to make her forgive me.

Six hours of backbreaking work numbed my brain and wreaked havoc on my body as I trudged back up the steps to the cabin. It was one am, and I'd watched the lights turn out in the living room hours ago and it had taken all I had inside of me to not come back then, sliding into bed against Hadley's warm body and using my body to distract her from all of my inadequacies.

Instead, I'd forced myself to stay outside in the cold for hours more until I was dead on my feet. I silently entered the house and motioned for Dev to stay where he was on the couch as I kicked off my boots and shed the layers of my protective clothing. The fire burned brightly, warming the living space, and casting a bright warm glow over the area, highlighting the beautiful woman who had stolen my desire to live alone in quiet torture like I had been doing for the last four years.

Hadley sat in the chair she loved in the corner by the fire, with her head tilted to the side and her knees to her chest, covered by the warm blanket I'd covered her with the first night she sat down there with me. She was asleep and my body ached to feel hers against it as I watched her silently.

"Fucking hell," I muttered and took off my shirt until I stood before her in only a pair of jeans and socks and slowly slid my arms under her body. She startled in her sleep, instinctively wrapping her arms around my neck at the sensation of being lifted as her eyes fluttered open and looked up at me in the darkness.

"Kip." She whispered, looking down at my bare chest and then back up into my eyes.

"I'm sorry," I said, unable to offer anything else. "Let me hold you tonight." I implored her, fearing that she would tell me to go to hell and deny me what I unreasonably asked of her. Instead, she just sighed and laid her head on my shoulder, taking a deep breath against my neck.

"I missed you." She breathed, and I could hear the gloom in her voice.

"I shouldn't have left. I just... wanted to give you space." As I cleared the top of the stairs and walked us into my bedroom, I elaborated, "But I can't stay away. Something about you pulls me in."

"You say that like it's a bad thing." She stated sadly as I gently laid her down in the center of my bed.

Our bed.

If she wasn't in it, I knew it would never beckon to me again.

"I know." Shedding my jeans, I nestled beside her and drew her body snugly against mine. "I don't mean to."

"You can't help if that's how you feel." She replied, settling her head on my chest and taking a deep breath. "I've never mattered to another human being even one time in my life, I shouldn't hope to start now."

"I don't want you to leave." Into the silence, I confessed, "I don't know how to be what you need me to be either."

She didn't respond as she laid in my arms, after a while she finally spoke. "I grew up in foster care." She paused, and I could tell she was fighting with herself to open up with me. "I've never belonged anywhere, or to anyone. I've never cared about it much either, because I could come and go as I pleased and didn't have to answer to anyone. So if this isn't where I'm supposed to be, then I'll move on, Kip."

There was no need for me to respond, as the silence hung heavy in the air, filled with unspoken words. The connection between us was going to fizzle out if I didn't come clean to her and she would not bear all to me unless I took the first step.

I just didn't know how to take one step without watching it all implode once I put things into motion.

Chapter 11 - Hadley

A few days later, we were in the same loop of activities like we weren't living on borrowed time. Kip left early to go out and do chores, leaving me alone in the house, once again.

I heard a plow go by the day before, but neither of us said anything about it out loud.

He didn't want me to go; he had said that the night I asked him about Molly. Since that night, he has shown me a gentler and kinder side of him. He woke me up each morning with his lips and hands and amazing cock and put me to sleep each night, exhausting me with the likes of him all over again. Yesterday, he didn't have too many chores to do, so he stayed inside with me, and we laid on the couch in front of the fire naked and made crazy slow love to each other like time didn't exist and neither did our pasts or our futures.

Yes, I was referring to it as making love. When he got that soft, magical look in his eyes, he would lay me down and worship my body like it was the temple of his every hope and dream. He was so attentive and giving and he pushed my body to orgasm over and over until I couldn't keep my eyes open long enough to do it again. And then we slept and woke up and did it all over again.

It wasn't like I really had anywhere else to go, anyway. Florida had been a diversion and an escape for me from the boring monotony of my life. But the idea of staying with Kip in his secluded forest wonderland... made my heart soar and made my worries fade.

Most of my worries.

When I was alone and free of any tasks, I allowed my head to drift back to the torture I'd endured just weeks ago. My bruises had mostly faded, some had turned yellow on the ugly side of healing, but they were fading, and with them went some of the fears and nightmares. The only two things that still plagued me awful much were the wounds to my left hand from the snare I'd learned was Kip's, and the broken ribs on both of my sides.

With time, both would also fade away, leaving only the memories to haunt me in silence. And then, I would almost be able to pretend none of it had happened.

But I'd never be free of it entirely. I was living in the same woods that had tortured me and I knew at some point I'd have to answer for what I had done. I had a feeling that it would come back and take my happily ever after away from me. Not once in life did I get the easy way out of something, and I wouldn't bet on that changing. Telling Kip was inevitable, and I knew I couldn't avoid it forever. He deserved to know the truth, even if he still hadn't told me anything about his past at all. We hadn't discussed it in days, and I felt weak for letting it go. But I couldn't stand seeing the pain in his eyes when it came up.

I was in love with him. Unapologetically in love with a man, I knew nothing about and had known for next to no time at all.

I hadn't wanted to love him. Hell, I didn't even want to like him when we first met. He was such a brooding asshole that treated me like shit when he bothered to treat me like I existed at all. I wanted to hate him and just get through the few days I had to stay at his place because of the snow, and then get on my way after he took me back to town and never think about him again.

But he made me fall in love with him. He forced his way deep into my soul and I wasn't strong enough to fight it like I had with everyone else. He tore down every defense I had by validating the intense connection between us, and I fell hard and fast and regretted not a second of it.

And I knew there was no way I could walk away from him and never look back. I just had to figure out how to stay without what I did, tearing us down and burning us to ashes.

I also had to figure out how to keep his past from getting in between us, too.

Hours ago, he'd gotten ready as soon as he got up and took off, letting the distance be physical and emotional between us again. The quiet in the house was amplified by the noise of the thoughts in his head. I was patient and tried to be respectful, giving him space and silent support.

But the silence was becoming deafening.

At noon, he came in for lunch, leading a tired and hungry Dev in for his bowl first before he searched out his own food. Fresh BLT sandwiches and soup already waited for us on the island.

But when he walked in and saw them, he just went to the pantry, got a couple of cans of tuna out, and went about making them. In more silence.

From where I sat on the stool, I asked quietly. "You don't like BLT's?" I had on another simple outfit of yoga pants and a zip-up athletic jacket, but I felt bare. I picked at a stray thread on the cuff of my sleeve as he just grunted and shrugged.

"If you'd tell me these things, I can try to make what you do like." I tried again.

"I don't like BLT's." He said gruffly from the fridge as he got mayo out.

"But you like bacon, lettuce, and tomato. Just not together? I thought everyone liked them."

"Well, I don't. Is that okay?" He snapped as he slammed the fridge door shut.

I flinched at the noise and closed my eyes to calm myself. He wasn't angry with me, I told myself. I was okay.

He stood at the counter and finished mixing his tuna before turning as he began eating it without sitting down.

He sighed as he saw me just sitting there, not eating. Like that annoyed him, too.

"You just don't make them like-" He cut himself off as I sat there waiting, praying, wishing for a tidbit of information from him. A small piece of his past, a crumb, anything! "Never mind." He sighed, turning his back to me as he finished eating, looking at the cabinet.

He would rather look at a cabinet than me.

I wasn't good enough.

Shame and pain roared through my veins as my heart sputtered and my body shivered. "Like Molly does?" I asked in a whisper.

He whipped around so fast I flinched again and had to grab the counter to keep from falling off the stool as I ground my teeth and waited for the slap or punch, but it didn't come. As soon as the words were out of my mouth, I regretted them. But I couldn't live in ignorant silence anymore. This was more than just a landing place for me on my way to somewhere else. He was more than just a man that was sheltering me until he could take me home. There was more between us, and I needed to know if I was a fool for believing he felt anything for me after he'd forced me to feel for him.

"That's what you were going to say, wasn't it?" I asked calmly. By keeping any trace of fear and anger out of my voice, I attempted to show him nothing but understanding and reason. "I just want to understand, Kip. I don't make them like Molly does, and that's why you don't like them."

"Don't say her name!" He commanded. "Don't you dare say her name."

"She's your wife, isn't she?" I asked, with more strength behind it. "You think I don't deserve to know if you're married? Or if at any point a woman is going to walk through the front door and want to know what the hell I'm doing in her house?"

He wouldn't answer me though, he just threw his bowl into the sink where the porcelain shattered against the stainless steel. I flinched again, but he didn't care. He marched past me to the front door, where he started putting his gear back on. He was just going to walk out and expect me to just sit here and be okay with it.

"I see you; you know." I breathed. He didn't stop lacing up his boots as I spoke, but I knew he was listening. "I see you every morning wake up and look around and for a brief second," I closed my eyes and shook my head slightly as I fought for composure, "just one second, I see the disappointment in your eyes when you see it's me next to you in bed." My voice trembled, and I battled to steady my breathing as I fought against the flood of emotions in my throat, finally opening my eyes again. He stopped moving as he just stood with his back to me, staring at the wall. I took a step closer to him, and the sound of my own footsteps echoed in the room. "It happens so fast, I can almost convince myself it didn't happen at all, and that I imagined the pain that the rejection causes inside of my heart. But then it happens again the very next morning, and the pain comes back like it never left to begin with."

He turned quickly and looked over his shoulder at me. Pain reflecting mine showed on his face, but I couldn't tell if it was pain for me or pain for himself. Opening my arms at my side, I bared my vulnerable self to him. "I didn't ask to be here, Kip. I didn't ask for you to want me or to feel guilty for it, either." With him at least looking at me, I attempted to reason with him.

Didn't he see my pain like I saw his? Didn't that soften him even a little? So I tried again.

"I didn't ask for any of this, but I can't just bury my head in the sand and hope that one day you'll wake up and find peace in your soul, that it's me next to you when you wake up like I do every single morning waking up in your arms. I can't wait around and just blindly hope for that Kip. If you can't tell me everything right now, at least tell me I'm not sticking around in a hopeless situation." I pleaded as I held my hands over my heart. "Please, just have mercy on me."

He still said nothing as I closed my eyes and dropped my head, wrapping my arms around myself, trying to hold it all together.

He walked over to me, closing the distance slowly. The moment our eyes met, I could sense my hope pouring out through my gaze. I could feel my body freeze up and hang on to what he was about to say.

But then he just did what he was good at.

He stayed silent.

He leaned down and kissed my cheek, not touching me anywhere other than where his lips seared my skin before he turned and walked back out the front door.

When the wood creaked beneath the force of the slam so powerful the walls rattled, I let out a shuttered breath and Dev bellowed from the front porch.

"It seems that my peace here has officially come to a close," I whispered to the silent house.

Occupying my brain with indoor chores, I picked up the mess from lunch and silently made plans.

As I stood in the laundry room, folding a load of laundry and packing my bag, I tried to come up with the words to tell him what I had done in his mountains, as a last resort to rescue the situation. But I knew if I did, he could ruin my life with that information. I found myself staring blankly at the closed door next to the bathroom, my mind racing with repetitive thoughts.

The only room in the house Kip had never shown me and the only one that he kept the door closed on. With trembling hands, I set the laundry down and cautiously approached the door. Peering down the long, empty hallway, I strained my ears for any hint of Kip or Dev's approach, but the silence remained unbroken. My pulse sped up as I stood there staring at the door handle for what felt like an eternity.

Something inside of me told me to walk away, that if he had wanted me to know what was in the room, he would have left the door open or told me about it.

But he hadn't even mentioned it, he acted as though the door didn't exist, and that made me feel like I needed to know what was on the other side of it.

I took a deep breath and then quickly reached down and turned the handle before I lost the nerve. My heart nearly exploded out of my chest when it turned and opened with hardly any effort. With one hand, I pushed the door open and stood frozen in the hallway, absorbing the scene before me.

Someone painted the walls pink and blue, separating the space into two halves. On the pink side, there was a white daybed with a pastel purple comforter on it, adorned with frills and lace, beneath hanging butterflies from the ceiling. On the blue side, baseball trophies and decor splattered haphazardly on the walls and furniture in true boy fashion.

It was a kids' room.

"My god," I whispered as I took in the sight of it.

Boxes were scattered in the center of the room with items hanging out of them and strewn across the floor as if someone had thrown them in here without a care.

As if on autopilot, my feet led me towards them, and I ended up in the middle of the room, peering down at the fascinating items.

Memories.

On top of one box was a photo frame with a broken glass front. I tipped the frame over and let the glass fall into the half-empty box below it. And there, framed in broken shards of glass and a busted wooden edge, was a picture of Kip. He looked younger, maybe by a couple of years, but he didn't have a beard or a scowl. Instead, he was clean-shaven and smiling from ear to ear back at the camera sitting on a log next to a campsite.

And the reason he looked the happiest I'd ever seen him was wrapped around him on all sides.

A beautiful blond woman stood behind him, with her arms around his shoulders, as she leaned down and kissed his cheek. And on each knee were two of the cutest kids I'd ever seen.

A boy and a girl.

The little boy was a spitting image of Kip, with his dark coloring and perfect smile. And the little girl was an exact replica of the gorgeous woman holding Kip like he was her grand prize in life.

Molly.

Molly, my one true love, my soulmate among imposters.

I trembled looking at the happy family and then looked up around the room.

He was a dad and a husband.

The man I had fallen in love with in such a short time had a family. My legs gave out, and I fell to my knees amongst Kip's past.

Pictures littered the boxes, tons of them.

Pictures of the kids and them, all happy and all madly in love.

My hands shook uncontrollably as I filtered through them. I felt like such a spectator looking at their happy memories from the outside, but I needed to know where they were, why they weren't here with him, and what happened to his perfect family.

Below some pictures in one of the boxes, there were a couple of velvet jewelry boxes and I picked one up, unsure of what would be inside. When it snapped open, there was a military medal inside, with the Marine Corps logo on the inscription.

Next to a couple more of the same things were a few pictures out of frames. They were pictures of Kip, with other men dressed in military uniforms overseas. One picture was of him in his dress uniform, spiffed up with his crisp white hat and shiny metals on display, and so much about him fell into place from there.

Tears fell from my eyes and landed on the pictures that had collected in my lap. He had wanted to know my deepest darkest secrets, the ones that would tear me open and cause my heart to hemorrhage right there in front of him, but yet he never told me he was a soldier, or a father, or a husband.

He was making plans for the house to help me get more comfortable here, all the while his kids' bedroom was locked away with pictures of them and his wife and all of his past like a tomb.

He wanted me to bear all of it to him when he couldn't even tell me the smallest part of his history. I felt so betrayed and heartbroken that there was this whole side of him I didn't know.

Did I know him at all?

"What the fuck do you think you're doing?"

I yelped and gasped as I turned towards the door in fear and shock at his harsh tone and words. The movement sent lightning bursts of pain up my sides and into my chest.

A sense of helplessness washed over me as he stood in the doorway, his scowl conveying nothing but disdain and fury.

I picked up the picture of them at the campsite and held it in front of him, my shoulders rising in shock and confusion, tears streaming down my face. I searched his eyes, silently pleading for him to say something that would bring clarity to the confusion.

It all had to have an explanation that I could understand.

It had to.

I needed it to make sense because I couldn't just accept that he had kept all of this hidden from me while lecturing me about honesty and lies.

"I asked what the fuck you were doing in here, Hadley!" He yelled from the doorway. His body was coiled tightly, his hands clenched into fists at his side, his chest heaving with anger, and I slid backward slightly away from his bulking form.

"Wh- what is all this?" I finally got out of my mouth. With my eyes wide in shock and mouth open, I just stared up at him. The events unfolding before me were so overwhelming that my mind couldn't comprehend them.

"It's none of your goddamn business! Get up." He ordered, but I couldn't get my body to move. I couldn't just get up and walk away from all of this. I looked down at the boxes and opened my arms, motioning to it all.

"How can you say it's none of my business? After what has happened between us here. How could you say that?" Instead of replying, he simply met my gaze, his eyes burning with a murderous rage. "What does all of this mean, Kip? Why is all of this in here shut away?" My entire body was shaking, and my lungs felt like I couldn't grasp my next breath fully as panic set in.

He bellowed over top of me, "Get out. Get up and get your shit and get the fuck out of my house." Now it was my turn to just stare back in horror. "I said get out!" He screamed as he lunged forward, grabbing me by the arm and yanking me up to my feet before turning and pulling me out of the room. He ripped the picture frame out of my hand and threw it at the wall where it exploded on impact, raining shards of glass and wood down on us.

Dragging me down the hall, he lifted my arm so high that I struggled to stay on my feet and had to fight to maintain my balance. "Stop. Kip, stop! You're hurting me!" A scream erupted from my lips as I crashed into the doorjamb, my shoulder slamming against the unforgiving wood, sending waves of agony coursing through me. "Kip!" I screamed again, but he didn't stop.

He let go of me once we got to the living room, and I tripped without his hand on my arm, falling into the back of the couch and landing on the floor in a heap.

My mind left the present and fell to the past in a similar situation I'd gotten myself into. The *Saint's* heinous words flowed over me once again, like he was in the very room.

Worthless little bitch. You think you're worth a damn thing? You're insignificant. Literally worth nothing. No one wants you. No one has ever wanted you.

My vision darkened around the edges as the pain overtook my entire body as memories flashed back, blocking out everything that was happening around me. I got sucked back into flashbacks, recalling my tortures.

"You dirty little slut. You should thank me for taking you into my home and sheltering you. Feeding you! Bathing you! You selfish, ungrateful cunt!" The Saint threw me to the floor before winding up and kicking me in the ribs when I landed. I screamed but nothing came out, the pain was so intense my vision darkened, and my hearing dulled until all I could hear was the roaring of his insults and the thuds of his kicks hitting my back and sides. I curled into a ball, trying to protect my head and stomach as he kicked me repeatedly. "You're going to appreciate me after a night outside in the ground! You'll be begging me to bring you back inside, you'll

lay on your back and spread your legs for me like the little whore I know you really are!"

I careened back to my present situation but couldn't differentiate the two. God, no. Please don't let Kip hit me. I won't survive it again.

Kip flew up the stairs to the loft, where I heard him slamming open the closet and drawers, getting my clothes, and throwing them into my bag. He came back down the stairs and threw the bag on the floor at my feet where I sat, hugging my knees to my front and sobbing.

"Get up. I'm taking you into town and you can figure out how to get the hell out of here and back to wherever the hell you came from, because I'm done. My past is none of your damn business. You wouldn't tell me what the fuck happened to you even though you came to me for help, so don't you dare get all high and mighty and demand that I tell you about me! You're a damn hypocrite." He yelled as he threw my coat and shoes at me as he stomped into his own.

"Pl- please Kip." I pleaded, trying to swallow my sobs. "Please, just talk to me, don't do this."

"Talk?" He yelled again. The veins in his face and in his neck were bulging from his anger. "I don't want to talk to you. You served your purpose while you were here. We had a good thing going, you warming my bed and giving me holes to shove my cock into, then you had to go and get nosey and snoop in shit that is none of your business and now we're here. This is your fault. You just couldn't leave well enough alone."

I didn't recognize the man in front of me anymore. He was saying such heinous things. "Don't be cruel, just tell me what's going on. I just want to know what's going on, why didn't you tell me about them?" I kept trying, even though my survival skills were telling me to run far away. He picked me up again by my arm, although he was gentler, he still lifted me off of my feet and caused me to stumble behind him towards the door.

"Put your shit on or I'm dragging you through the snow barefoot." He snapped as he pulled me to face him. He leaned down and got right into my face, "Unless you'd rather walk to town on your own again. It should be getting dark soon, so you should feel right at home walking all alone out there." He grabbed my coat from my hands and forced my arms into it roughly. "Right, Hadley? When you ended up on my property, weren't you just out enjoying the winter wonderland?"

His face morphed into a mocking glare. "Oh wait, you don't want to talk about what happened to you though, right? You haven't wanted to talk about it once, but you expect me to just let you into all of my personal shit like it doesn't matter, like it's not relevant because you had it worse. Like my family is less important than whatever happened to you? Is that what you think?" He sneered at me again as he grabbed my legs and forced my shoes onto my feet haphazardly. "My dead family is less important than you getting roughed up by some boyfriend. Like their murders mean less than your bruised ribs and busted lip!"

Murders? Oh God!

"I didn't say that!" I pleaded. He ripped the door open and shoved me out of it, I stumbled again and fell on my knees onto the hardwood of the porch. "Kip! Stop, please!" I yelled as more tears fell from the pain in my hand contacting the ground.

"Kip?" I looked up from where I was on my knees in the snow on the porch to see a man standing at the bottom of the stairs looking up at me and then at Kip in pure disbelief. "What's going on here, boy?"

I looked at the man in horror; at how I knew the scene looked, but he just walked up the steps and stood between me and Kip, who stood in the doorway with as much horror and a lot of guilt on his face.

"Not now, Mike. Now's not a good time. I'm taking her into town, and I'll be back later."

The man, Mike, looked to be in his fifties, with salt and pepper hair and beard, dressed in a red flannel and jeans much like Kip. He said nothing, but leaned down and offered me his hand to help me stand up. I tentatively placed my good hand in his and he gently picked me up.

He was tall and broad like Kip, not as big, but I could tell he was not to be messed with either, and it gave me a bit of relief to know he had stopped Kip's tirade.

His anger was clearly pain and fear resurfacing now that I knew what had happened to his family, but he still terrified me. I had my own trauma too.

"You okay?" Mike asked me, ignoring what Kip had said.

I nodded my head gently, looking down at the ground as I brushed some of the snow off of me. It was already seeping into my clothes and chilling me.

Memories of how cold I had been when I was forced to sleep in the hole in the ground and the days I spent walking flooded my mind. I trembled in fear, never wanting to experience that level of coldness again.

"Let's go inside and get you dried off, darling," Mike said, ignoring Kip's protests and opening the door to lead me through it. I looked up at Kip in question and the look of disgust that he aimed my way stopped me in my tracks. He didn't want me in his home anymore.

"No," I whispered. They both looked down at me as I stepped back and away from them. "I'm not welcome here anymore. I'm fine, but I just want to leave."

Mike looked from me to Kip and then back before reaching forward once again and gently leading me into the still open front door. "I'll take you myself in just a minute, but first I need to have a word with Kip. Go on inside and warm yourself by the fire and we'll be on our way in just a little bit."

He didn't give me much choice as he ushered me in and shut the door behind me with gentle authority. Unable to move and unable to process what had happened, I stood on the inside in shock.

Sagging against the kitchen counter, grabbing a stool to fall into as the weight of everything nearly made me collapse. I could hear the guys on the other side of the door, and I quieted my breathing to listen to them.

"What exactly is going on here?" Mike asked angrily.

Kip sighed heavily and I could imagine him running his hand over his beard before rubbing the back of his neck as he usually did in frustration.

"Nothing. She needs a ride to town. Nothing else."

"Who is she?"

"It's a long story, Mike, one I don't have the time to indulge you in right now. I'm going to take her into town and then I'll be back."

"Like hell I'm letting her get in a vehicle with you right now, I already told you I'd take her down. Now tell me, did you leave those bruises on her face and neck, boy?"

"Do you really think I'd do that, Mike?" Kip sounded wounded by the older man's words.

"Do you realize what I just saw when I pulled up?" Mike asked loudly, "I could hear you screaming at her from way out here, then you blew through the door and shoved her down the steps onto her hands and knees. That poor girl is as small as a sack of flour and you put your hands on her and threw her down like a rag doll. The look of fear in her eyes nearly stopped my heart, I can't even imagine how she feels. I don't care what she did to rile you up so badly, but no woman deserves that.

And the Kip I've known since he was a boy would never touch a woman like that for a second, let alone yell at her in that tone or say such vile things. So right now I can't tell you what I think you're capable of. I do know I haven't seen you this pissed off since you got home five years ago, so you want to try that line again and actually tell me what the hell is going on?"

Kip sighed once again and started pacing on the porch. "She's just someone I've been- well, we've been fooling around. And today I found her snooping around in the kids' bedroom, looking through pictures of Molly and the kids and I just- I lost my damn mind." He paused as he kept pacing. "Fuck, Mike, I put my hands on her. Fuck!" He yelled and kicked the chair on the deck. "I hadn't told her anything about them and then I found her in there and she was upset about finding out that way and I just—I lost it."

"Well, you fucked up, that's for sure. How'd she get all the bruises and the busted hand if not from you?"

I got up and walked over to the kitchen window, so I could see them and watch what was going on.

"No fucking clue, man," Kip said as he shook his head and threw his hands up in surrender. "Seriously. Two weeks ago, I found her with her hand caught in one of my snare traps, about two miles out from here, beaten, bloody, unconscious, and frozen half to death. When she woke up, she didn't even know what state she was in and wouldn't tell me who beat her up. Can't get a damn thing out of her other than her name is Hadley, and she grew up in foster care in New York City."

"Hadley?" Mike looked towards the front door with a shocked look on his face before looking back at Kip. My heart sank as I saw the array of emotions cross the older man's face. "No fucking way." He muttered and then he took off barreling towards the front door, with Kip hot on his heels.

"What? What's wrong?" Kip asked as Mike stormed through the front door and turned to face me with disbelief written all over his face.

I stood still as stone, at the kitchen sink, watching the unraveling of my life happen right before my eyes.

"Hadley? Hadley Shaw? From New York?" Mike asked, rapid-firing questions at me. But I couldn't answer. I couldn't nod, I couldn't do anything but grip the edge of the sink in horror as I tried to keep from passing out.

He knew.

And I was going to pay for what I'd done.

"What's going on Mike?" Kip asked, but we paid no attention to him as our focus was on each other, so he attempted once more. "I'm not kidding Mike. Tell me what's going on, you're worrying me."

Mike ignored him again, questioning in disbelief. "There's no way. You're hardly bigger than a kid. There's no way you could have done that kind of damage to a man that size." Mike said as he looked me up and down at the way I was cradling my hand and my sides.

Kip looked over at me, his eyes wide with confusion and speculation, but I still couldn't say anything. I just felt more tears pool in my eyes before dropping over my eyelashes to my cheeks where they ran down them silently. Kip grabbed Mike from the shoulders and forcefully turned him to face him head-on. "What are you talking about!" He yelled.

With a skeptical expression, Mike turned to me again, then glanced at Kip. "She murdered Pastor Daniels," he stated firmly, his voice laced with disbelief.

Chapter 12 - Kip

I n an instant, the noise in the room vanished, and all that remained was the deafening sound of my blood rushing through my veins. I dropped my hands from Mike's shoulders and stumbled backward slightly, as though he had hit me.

She murdered Pastor Daniels.

Murder.

I looked over at Hadley and saw the guilt written all over her face, confirming that what he had said was true.

"No," I said, shook my head, and stepped back further. "No way. There's no way I've been fucking a murderer!" It couldn't be true.

Murderers took my family away, there's no way I could have given aid to one.

She recoiled at my words, eyes closing as more tears fell down her face. She cried so much.

Mike cleared his throat from next to me, speaking to her with more calmness than I had. "Police are looking for you, Hadley. They found your blood at the crime scene, and hounds followed your trail for a way. There's a manhunt going on as we speak. How did you make it this far? We're almost fifteen miles from the Pastor's property."

I yelled out before she had a chance to answer, "Tell me what happened." I demanded. There was a level of anger in my voice that alarmed even me. "Pastor Daniels was a good man! He was kind and helped everyone he came across and you killed him? How? I want answers and I want them right the fuck now, Hadley!"

Her eyes snapped open and for the first time since I'd met her, there was anger in them. "Kind?" With incredulity, she asked. She opened her arms wide, revealing herself, "Do I look like he was *kind* to me?" She screamed. "You saw all the bruises, and cuts and burns, the handprints around my throat! He tortured me, Kip! To the point where I begged for death. I pleaded with that devil himself to take me, to end the anguish, and you dare call him kind?" She spat out the last word like it tasted bad on her tongue.

No. She was wrong.

"I don't believe you. You lied the second you woke up here and you haven't stopped lying since then and you're lying now. You have to be lying. That man was loved by everyone that met him, there's no way he could have beat you. And all I know right now is that I found you in the woods, covered in blood!" I yelled, taking a large step towards her.

Mike put his hand on my shoulder, holding me back from getting any closer to her.

But she stepped closer in her own anger. "And bruises! You found me covered in blood and bruises! You have no idea the horrors I survived at the hands of that monster." She bit out, her face contorting as she pointed her finger at my chest angrily. "I survived because he didn't. He was going to kill me. He told me that every single day. That man didn't just beat me, Kip. You keep saying I was beat up, roughed up a little by some dude, but it was so much more than that. I was tortured in ways you wouldn't even have tortured terrorists overseas!"

No, that didn't make sense! I grabbed my hair and pulled it as I paced in frustration before turning back to her once more, "No! You're wrong! You murdered someone! A good man!" I felt an eerie, menacing calm settle over my body as I let my disgust fall from my lips at her. "You're no better than the pieces of scum that murdered my family and I pray to God you rot in jail until they put the needle in your arm and kill you for what you did."

She gasped at my accusation and recoiled back, swallowing down the pain. It was the most fucked up thing I'd ever said before. I instantly knew that even before Mike stepped forward and stood between us.

"Okay, I think that's enough for right now, you are both upset about what happened earlier and now this is a lot of stress on top of that-" He tried to reason but I could see the finality on Hadley's face as she wiped harshly at the tears on her face in anger.

"You know what, Kip?" She said as she stared at me unwaveringly, "I wish I had told you everything right away. Because then, you would have hated me instantly and called the police and I never would have fallen in love with you."

My heart stopped beating when she said the words. Until today I'd thought myself to be falling in love with her, but to hear her say it made me know I had been. But she wasn't done.

"I'd walk back into the Hell that deranged Saint inflicted on me with open fucking arms if it would take back every single thing that happened between us. I'd face him again if it'd make meeting you never happen because just like that, you've leveled the playing field for me by reminding me you have all the power and obviously the capabilities to hurt me physically and emotionally, just like *he* did!" She threw her arms up in frustration, "You are just like him, maybe even worse. Because the entire time he was hurting me, he told me he was going to, he told me over and over how he'd end my life, but not until he'd destroyed every single part of my soul first. But you tricked me into thinking I was safe here with you while you were the one who actually finally destroyed me."

There was no way Peter Daniels had hurt her the way she was describing. There had to be an explanation, maybe we were talking about two different people.

But as I looked down at her in silence, I realized she had never lied to me. She didn't tell me the truth, but she had never lied. I deflated, the adrenaline having run its course through my veins, leaving me exhausted and bewildered. I had seen the marks on her body firsthand, saw the pain she was in physically and emotionally, and if she said that Pastor Daniels had done it to her, didn't she deserve to be believed? Why would she lie? She couldn't have lied about the marks; I had seen them.

I turned to look at Mike, searching his face for some clue, but found he was struggling the same as me. "For God's sake, there were handprints around her fucking throat. Multiple sets." I said to him, looking for some way to explain all of it. But the answer to all of it was on his face and I realized then that I'd had it the entire time. Someone had beaten the proof into her body until she was nearly crippled with it, and I had it all along.

I paced back and forth in the kitchen with my hands pulling on my hair as I tried to figure out what to do. The police were after Hadley, but I couldn't let them just arrest her. She'd been traumatized too much already; it would destroy her to be treated like a criminal after what happened to her. Fuck, I still didn't even know what exactly happened to her other than somehow she'd come in contact with Peter, and he'd beaten her repetitively until she somehow managed to kill him. And then she walked nearly fifteen miles in the freezing cold before I found her. There was a reason I'd found her, that she had ended up on my property. I was supposed to protect her, and I'd done the exact opposite when she needed me the most.

I whipped around again to face her, "Hadley-"

But the words died on my lips when I saw her staring back out the window with fear in her eyes. I looked past her and saw three sheriff's cars pulling up my driveway.

She slowly turned to face me with complete defeat in her eyes and her shoulders slumped as reality set in.

And for the rest of my years on earth, I'll never forget the catastrophic pain on her face as she looked at me and whispered, "I guess it's time for me to get the needle for what I've done."

"No," I said when I watched past her as Sheriff Boyd got out of his car, flanked by two deputies. I rushed toward her and spun her to face me, but she wouldn't look at me. She just hung her head in defeat. "Listen to me." I tilted her head up and bent down until she was looking at me. Her eyes were bloodshot and swollen from crying for so long, but her face was devoid of any emotion other than loss. "I'm sorry," I said, tilting her head up and bending down until she was looking at me. Her eyes were bloodshot and swollen from crying for so long, but her face showed no emotion other than loss. "My family was taken from me five years ago while I was away at war, and I've never dealt with it. Having you here forced me to decide if I could let them go for good or watch you walk out of my life. I came back in here earlier to tell you that you weren't wasting your time here with me, that I just needed time to figure out how to love both the past and the present and then I found you in there, and you were distraught, and I lost my mind. I'm so sorry." Breathing her in, I placed my forehead against hers. She placed her hands on my chest and gripped my shirt, holding onto me. "But I believe you. Dammit, Had, I believe you. I don't understand why this happened to you or how, but I believe it did. And I'll do everything in my power to help you clear your name. Baby, I can pull strings and call in favors with the police. I believe you." In a state of frenzy, I attempted to express everything as quickly as possible. I could hear the heavy footsteps of the cops on the porch and knew I was out of time.

"Me too, Ms. Hadley. I'll help in any way I can because I can see the truth in your eyes. I believe you too." Mike said from behind me as the door vibrated with knocking from the outside.

She remained silent and wouldn't look at either of us as she just hung her head.

"Kip? It's Sheriff Boyd, I need your help with something." The sheriff called out from the porch.

Mike stepped forward and put his hand on the door handle as he turned to look at us. Stepping forward and standing just in front of her to the side, I turned to face him as I reached down and pulled Hadley's tiny ice-cold hand into mine. I knew what needed to happen, but I was going to protect her the best I could while it did.

With a single nod from me, Mike opened the door and nodded briefly to the sheriff, who shifted his gaze between him and me, before finally looking down at the petite pixie standing behind me, holding my hand.

Sheriff Boyd paused for a second before he stepped forward over the threshold, removing his hat and addressing me. "You want to tell me why you're holding the hand of a fugitive wanted for murder, Kip? Pretty little thing that she is," He paused, taking her in from head to foot, "but wanted for murder, nonetheless."

I pulled her behind me further as I leveled him with a stare that made better men sweat and he recoiled slightly. He wasn't a bad man, but I didn't appreciate the way he eyed Hadley up and commented on her looks. "We didn't realize she was wanted until about five minutes ago when Mike told us. We've been snowed in until recently, and I don't have cable or anything up here," I clarified.

He nodded his head and stepped into my home further, making room for his two deputies. I didn't miss how the young one who looked like he'd just graduated from the academy put his hand on the pistol on his hip and looked at her as though Hadley was going to reach out and strike like an animal.

"You'd better get your hand off that gun inside of my home boy, before you truly need it." I warned him, staring him down.

"Kip." The sheriff and Mike warned cautiously. I couldn't help it, though. My body was wound up tight and if anyone was going to lash out at the deputies, it was going to be me. And I could sure as hell do a lot more damage than she could.

"You'd be singing a different tune, Mr. Montgomery, if you'd seen the way she gutted that nice pastor in his own home. Carved him up like he was some piece of scrap meat." The young buck sneered, never taking his eyes off of her from where she stood behind me.

I took a menacing step towards him as my lip curled up in disgust at his sniveling weak self, but Hadley grabbed the back of my shirt, pulling me back again.

"No, don't." She said as she dropped my hand and stepped out in front of me. "My name is Hadley Catherine Shaw, you're here for me, leave him out of it."

"There's a warrant out for your arrest in connection to the murder of Peter Daniels, Ms. Shaw. I came here only to ask Kip if he'd seen anything unusual, seeing as how your trail had pointed in this direction before we lost it. I never expected to find you here though, that's for sure. Or looking the way you do, either." The sheriff said as he eyed Hadley speculatively, taking in what he could of her bruises on the skin that was bare to his gaze before looking up at me again.

"Hadley, say nothing until my lawyer gets here," I warned from behind her, I moved forward again and laid my hand on her shoulder to show her I was right there with her. Without uttering a word, she shrugged my hand off her shoulder and continued walking, her footsteps echoing as she grabbed her bag from the floor next to the cabinet.

"I don't want a lawyer, Mirandize me and handcuff me if it makes you feel better and take me to the station." She said, speaking to the sheriff only.

"Hadley, you don't know what you're saying. Just take a deep breath and protect yourself, okay? Just think about this and let me help you." I pleaded, putting my hands on both shoulders now.

Sheriff Boyd hadn't made any move towards her and neither had his cohorts, but the threat of them putting iron on my girl's wrists kept me on edge.

Hadley turned to me and leveled me with her stare. "I don't want your help, Kip. Don't pull any strings or call in any favors, don't call your lawyer, and sure as hell don't try to visit me in jail. You've made your feelings incredibly clear today. You think I'm a murderer and you lost your family to someone like that and that should be all that has to be said." She turned back to the cops then. "Are you going to arrest me officially, or are you just going to make me stand in the middle of the house from which I was told to get out ten minutes ago?"

"No, just stop for a second. I was wrong-" I started.

"Please." She begged the sheriff, acting like I wasn't even in the room anymore.

Sheriff Boyd hung his head like he wasn't super happy about what he was about to do as he stepped forward, releasing his handcuffs from his belt.

"Hadley Shaw, you're under arrest for the murder of Peter Daniels. Anything you say can and will be used against you in a court of law. You have the right to-" I didn't hear anything else as I stood watching in shock as he handcuffed her hands behind her back and led her out my front door.

Out of my home.

Away from me.

Chapter 13 - Hadley

T he metal around my wrists was cold.

Cold like the air.

Like my skin had become.

Like my heart had gone.

Cold seeped into my veins like ice water leaving behind brittle fibers and frozen glass that shattered when the door to the police cruiser was shut behind me.

While they were leading me out, Kip stood frozen in the kitchen. I'd fought to remain composed as I put one foot in front of the other on the way to the cruiser. Just like I had walked through the woods when I was cold, alone, and afraid.

Yet there I was again. Cold, alone, and afraid.

I had felt warmth during my time with Kip. He had warmed me inside and out. We had a rocky start and a catastrophic ending, and while the time we had together was brief, I wouldn't give it back for anything.

Regardless of what I'd said in anger earlier, I was glad I'd met Kip Montgomery. He had healed me when I didn't even know how broken I was.

But it would be easier with a clean break. It would make it easier for him.

There was a very good chance I wasn't going to get away with what I had done, and I didn't want Kip dragged down with me through it.

He had suffered enough; he had suffered actual loss when his family was taken from him. The amount of suffering he had experienced was enough.

It was nothing compared to that.

I was nothing.

I'd never been anything to anyone a single day of my life.

I let him believe I was done, so he would be done. He had wanted me gone before it all came to light. He had been so mad and so hurt and had wanted me far, far away from him.

So I was giving him that, even after he realized how wrong he had been.

When the young cop shut the door behind me, Kip barreled out of the front door, running towards the car. Mike ran after him, grabbing him, trying to contain him as the young cop scrambled to get in the car and lock the door before Kip got to him. But Kip wasn't coming after him.

He was coming after me.

He slammed his fists against the window, calling out for me to stop it, to not do it, pleading with me to let him help.

But there was no help for me.

Right before the cop pulled away from the chaotic scene as Mike lost his hold on him, I turned and looked at him through the bars of the window. I saw his face contort in pain and fear, and it broke my heart to witness a man as strong as him break.

He was frantically trying to get to me. Screaming and yelling through the glass, panicking as the end of my nightmare unfolded right before him.

The end of one nightmare. The beginning of another.

"Goodbye," I said, just as the car pulled away, leaving him standing in the driveway.

Turning in my seat as the car took me down the lane, I made the mistake of watching in horror as he fell to his knees with his head hung in agony.

I'd broken the strongest man I'd ever met.

The only man I had ever loved.

The only man I would ever love.

I rode in silence to the police station as anguish rolled through my entire system. I knew what awaited me there, and it was something I didn't know if I could survive.

As we drove through town, the sight of a quaint small town filled with media vans and police agency vehicles on every corner surprised me.

When we got to the police station, TV cameras and federal agents instantly swarmed the car. They roughly yanked me from the car and propelled me through the crowd. I didn't hang my head in shame like you always see criminals do when they were led from the cop car to the station.

Instead, I looked up to the clear blue sky and tried to pretend I was on the beach in Florida and that none of it had happened.

They pulled my elbows to the front of my chest to get me into the station quickly, causing my body to ache and scream out in pain. I had to grind my teeth together to keep from crying out, but I wouldn't show my weakness out in the public.

I was stronger than that.

A life of growing up on the streets and in horrible foster homes made me stronger than that.

Everyone stared at me as I walked through the halls of the station. Police stopped what they were doing, mid-sentence, mid-bite of dinner, and just stared at me. I could see the shock and disbelief on their faces as I walked by, but I wasn't sure what part they were surprised by.

Was it the fact that I was tiny, at just two inches over five feet, and that I'd been capable of killing a man over six feet tall and pushing two hundred and fifty pounds? Or the fact that bruises marred every inch of my skin still and that wasn't what they had expected to see on a cold-blooded killer's body.

I was quickly ushered into a large interrogation room, with the young cop leading the way and FBI agents trailing closely behind.

My feet stopped moving when the door closed behind me as I looked around at the generic table with 4 chairs and the large mirror on the wall that no doubt had a room full of people on the other side of it. It was all unbelievable.

I was supposed to be on a beach in Florida.

No, I was supposed to be in Kip's warm cabin getting dinner ready for him.

The young cop grabbed my elbow roughly and jerked me forward again, my lungs exploded with pain, and I gasped in agony. "Please stop ripping my arms around. My ribs are broken!" I pleaded, but he just sneered at me as he threw me down into the chair before lifting my handcuffed hands up over the back of the chair, forcing my chest down onto the table. I hissed through my teeth and whimpered pathetically, even though I tried my hardest to hold it in.

Tears burned behind my finally dry eyes, so I shut them to hold them in. When he uncuffed my right hand, he ripped the left one to the side and attached the empty cuff to the bolt on the metal table, shackling me to the stationary object. The two FBI agents flanked the room, watching silently as he brutalized my already weakened body.

Whatever happened to innocent until proven guilty?

A moment later, the sheriff walked in with a couple more people, making the room feel small.

"Carlson, if I catch you roughing up a prisoner like that again, especially an injured one, I'll take you out back and teach you a lesson you won't be quick to forget. Do I make myself clear?" The older sheriff asked while staring down the rookie with disdain. The young pup nodded in silence before sneering at me once again. "Get out of here and go do your paperwork."

There was a middle-aged woman with him that wore the typical pant suit outfit of a superior and I could tell she was in charge of the interrogation almost immediately. She sat down across from me, Sheriff Boyd sat next to her, and two higher-up agents flanked them where the other two had stood before they left with the young Carlson.

The woman spoke first. "Hadley, I'm Special Agent Harvey, you've met Sheriff Boyd already." I didn't know what she wanted me to say, so I simply nodded. "You were read your rights and previously declined legal representation," she said, "Do you still wish to decline a lawyer at this time?"

"Yes," I answered evenly.

She nodded, looking slightly pleased with herself like it was going to make her job easier. But perhaps she didn't realize that I had been a paralegal studying under an incredible defense attorney at one of the most prestigious law firms on the East Coast before everything happened. I knew enough to get through.

"Okay, then let's get started." There was a camera on the wall with its little red light blinking, watching me and I shivered as I remembered another little blinking red light that had watched me.

It had always watched; it had seen everything.

Agent Harvey began laying a file folder down in front of her and withdrawing large photos of the man I'd killed, laying them down on the table between us, but I refused to look down at them. I already knew what he had looked like when I was done. "Peter Daniels was found murdered from multiple stab wounds inside of his home four days ago. Investigators discovered your DNA and fingerprints at the crime scene, specifically on the knife still embedded in his neck and inside his vehicle. I'm officially charging you with his murder at this point. We'd like to ask you some questions to get the bigger picture, including why you'd want to kill the man."

She paused, eyeing me accusingly, and then continued. "He's known throughout the community here as a good man and helpful leader." She sat back in her chair and adjusted her suit jacket, crossing her legs under the table in a show of authority, a move I'd seen played many times before. "But, on the other hand, you've had previous encounters with the law, haven't you?" She flipped a few pages in the file and read off a sheet, "Theft, breaking and entering, trespassing, assault." She tsked her teeth and cocked her head before looking back up at me. "Growing up in the sewers of New York City, bouncing from different group homes, and then out on your own at eighteen. I'd like to start with when you first met each other. How did the little street girl from New York and the nice kind preacher from Utah meet?" She held nothing back as she interrogated me, she knew which buttons to push, and my past was one of them.

Just as I was about to respond, a sudden knock on the door interrupted me. The agent swiftly opened it and stepped aside, revealing a face I immediately recognized. The first familiar face I had seen in weeks.

"Tim?" I asked pensively.

"I'm sorry, who are you?" Agent Harvey said as she stood up in annoyance.

"Timothy Jenks. I'm Ms. Shaw's lawyer and I will be representing her during questioning."

"What are you doing here?" I asked in pure shock.

Agent Harvey cut me off as she rounded on Tim, blocking my view of him. "Ms. Shaw has declined legal representation, Mr. Jenks; you need to leave this room immediately."

"She declined representation because I wasn't here yet. But I am now, and now she wants her lawyer." He said pointedly at me as he leaned around her and gave me a 'you listen here' look.

"You can't just barge in here and talk for her, we do not know who you are!" Harvey was getting worked up as she saw her easy conviction slipping through her fingers now that a high paid lawyer was present. And everyone knew he was A-list just by looking at him. He was an incredibly well aged man at sixty. He wore an Armani tailored three-piece suit and had an essence of class and poise that surrounded him wherever he went. Even in the most stressful courtrooms, he always kept his cool and maintained composure. He was someone I'd studied, and I had learned so much from working under him at his firm in New York, and, to be honest, having him in the room gave me some relief.

But why was he present?

How?

"My name is Timothy Jenks, I've already introduced myself, Special Agent, so may I suggest you pay better attention to minor details unless you hope I will do your job for you. However, I will close this case either way with my client being cleared of all charges." He turned and walked over to my side of the table. "Now, I'm going to ask you all politely to leave the room and turn off the mirror and camera so I may counsel my client and I'm also going to tell you, though I'm not going to be as polite about it, to unhandcuff her immediately as she's here of her own free will and is injured as you can clearly see."

I just stared in awe, as did everyone else in the room, as he unbuttoned his suit jacket and sat down next to me, while never letting his gaze slip off the Agent.

Sheriff Boyd cleared his throat with guilt as he walked around the table and undid the cuff. He wouldn't meet my eyes as he did so, though.

"You have five minutes, and then we're going to start this interrogation regardless if you're ready or not." Agent Harvey said before huffing her way out of the room followed by the agents.

Sheriff Boyd hung back until they were out of the room before he turned and looked at me finally. "I gave Kip permission to watch from the other room." He said as he looked towards the mirror.

"Make him leave. I don't want him here." I replied before lowering my voice, hoping Kip couldn't hear it through the mirror. "I don't want him to hear what I'm going to have to say. Shield him from it." I pleaded with him, using my eyes.

But just then the door opened forcefully and there stood the big brute of a man I'd tried to protect.

"Shield me?" He bellowed as he rounded the table. "God, you are so fucking stubborn. Don't think I don't know what that little stunt at the house was about. I get it, you're trying to protect me from the fallout of all of this, but you have to stop. You don't have to do everything on your own anymore, Hadley. Stop fighting and pushing me away." His face was grief-stricken under his anger and it aged his beautiful features.

I shook my head sadly as I looked down at my hands in my lap. "An hour ago you were telling me to get the fuck out of your life, Kip. You're not ready to deal with all of this. You obviously harbor way too many unresolved pains from your past to deal with this in the present."

"Hadley," Tim interrupts. "We only have four minutes left and you have a lot to fill me in on before they come back. I appreciate your dilemma here, but we need to handle that first so you can handle this after." He said, looking down at me kindly.

Sheriff Boyd left the room, leaving me, Tim, and Kip alone.

I took a deep breath and looked over at Tim. Ripping the band-aid off, "He kidnapped me from New York City the night I left for Florida. Used some injectable sedative to get me here. I was here six days before I almost escaped. He caught me and he tried to kill me with a knife, and I fought back. He died, and I took off." I turned back to look at Kip, who was hanging on my every word. "Kip found me two days later buried in the snow with death clawing at my back. He saved my life, but I never told him what happened. He's innocent, he knew nothing about it."

Tim nodded, processing the short version. "Okay." He said, placing his big palm on my shoulder and pulling me into a hug. "I'm going to get you out of this, Hadley. I promise."

He never made promises unless he was completely confident he could deliver.

Kip cleared his throat from behind me, and I pulled out of Tim's arms, turning to him.

"How do you know each other?" Kip asked as he sized up Tim.

Tim chuckled from next to me. "I'm a partner at the most prestigious law firm on the East Coast and Hadley is my head paralegal. She's brilliant and makes sure I look good at each court appearance. Or at least she did before she quit to move to Florida." His face saddened as he looked away from Kip and back to me. "When the FBI showed up at the firm looking for you I followed them here and set up shop at the hotel. I knew something happened and that what they were saying wasn't true and if you were going to be arrested, I was going to be here to protect you when you did."

"Thank you, Tim. Truly."

Kip moved closer to me and kneeled down next to my chair, drawing my attention back to him.

"You have to stop pushing me away. I'm sorry for everything I said. I was so incredibly wrong, and I can never take it back or make it right. But please don't push me away right now, let me be here for you and lean on me." He paused as he looked at Tim over my shoulder, before leaning in closer and said, "My alpha is hungry."

I cracked a smile at his joke, and he brought his hands up to cup my face as he leaned his forehead against mine, breathing me in. "My *bambina*." He whispered before kissing me softly. It felt incredible to be in his arms again. Earlier, when he had been so mad at me, my emotions were in ruins and the grief of losing him devastated me. I didn't forgive him for acting the way he did when he found me inside his kid's room, but as Tim said earlier, we had to handle the bigger problem before any of that mattered.

The door banged open, and Agent Harvey and her posse walked back in, breaking up the first moment of true calmness I'd had in hours.

"Kip, go on back next door." Sheriff Boyd said, and Kip sauntered out, keeping his eyes on me the whole way.

"Big guy, you got there." Tim joked from next to me. I smiled and looked at him before shrugging in answer. "The alpha." It was all I had to say to describe Kip.

When everyone got settled, I looked back up at the camera in the corner and watched the little red light turn back on.

They were watching again.

Chapter 14 - Hadley

The Grave

Agent Harvey wasted no time and started asking the questions as soon as she was settled. "When did you first meet Peter Daniels?"

I took a deep breath and began. "When I was sixteen. He volunteered at a youth shelter I stayed in occasionally."

"And what was your relationship with him, then?"

"Nothing. He mentored some kids who stayed there. I never stuck around long enough to interact with him. He tried a couple of times, wanted me to know that living on the street wasn't the only option I had, but I wasn't receptive and only stayed one night at a time every couple of months when I was in between places."

I knew oversharing could be dangerous, but I was trying to give them the complete answer.

"When was the last time you saw him before this time?"

"I stopped going to the shelter when I turned eighteen, so before that."

"How did your paths cross this time?" she asked.

What a nonchalant way of putting it. "He recently hired Jenks and Sawyer Law Firm, Tim's firm, where I worked, to represent him for a case. Maybe three months ago. He was working with one of the junior associates, so I didn't have any interaction with him other than in passing through the building."

"What had he hired the firm for?" She asked. I noticed the way her right eye twitched slightly as she asked it. I held her stare for a minute, staying silent because even I knew she couldn't ask that before she looked over at Tim.

"What a rookie cop question, Agent Harvey. At least try to make yourself look like you're not fishing for information we both know you don't have access to. Hadley wasn't privy to that knowledge as my paralegal, and even if she was, it's confidential under the legal representation clause. You'll have to subpoena the firm if you want to know that." Tim answered for me.

She huffed and held her head up as she straightened her spine and adjusted her jacket, "Did you two have any conversations while working at the firm?"

"He stopped me once in the lobby. A month ago, he said he recognized me as one of his girls from the shelter." I threw air quotes up at his name for me, "Like he'd had some sort of relationship with me back then. He asked me how I was doing, I told him I didn't remember him and that I was late for court and left. I didn't like the vibe I got off of him, so I told Tim and he told security to monitor him."

"What vibe was that?" She asked pensively. She leaned back and crossed her arms across her chest. Almost like she was showing me she was judging me and didn't believe my version of it.

"Like we were close; like we were old pals when, in reality, I had never said more than ten words to the man before."

"Okay, let's fast forward. How did you come to be in his home here in Utah?"

Instantly, images and memories from his home flooded my system. My pulse picked up, and I fought to control my emotions, even as I felt the red flush of anger creep up my face.

"I was at The Port Authority in the city, waiting to board a bus for Florida, where I was moving to. It was the middle of the night, my trip was a red eye, I went to use the bathroom in the main terminal, but it was closed for cleaning. So I went to use a secondary one by the main drop-off area." I paused then. Trying to articulate my words through the panic, I felt just talking about him. "By the time I saw him, it was already too late. I was at the sink washing my hands when he ran up behind me and smashed my face into the mirror. I fought back, clawing at him, kicking and elbowing anything I could get a hold of, but I couldn't get his grip out of my hair. He threw me to the ground and sat on my back with his knee between my shoulder blades and put a cloth over my nose and mouth. Then everything went black."

Panic swelled in my heart.

Deep breath Hadley, just breathe.

It was like I could hear Kip in my head, coaching me to stay calm.

"Then what?" She asked.

I swallowed the bile threatened to rise in my throat, "I woke up tied down in the back of an SUV. All the seats were gone and there was a mattress on the floor. He stopped at a rest stop, and I woke up, it was nighttime again. He said we'd made good time." I said bitterly. "Like we were on a road trip."

"Do you know what rest stop? Was there anyone around?"

"I don't know, I was tied down in the back. I couldn't see anything out of the windows other than the sky."

"What happened at the rest stop?" Her tone changed slightly as she asked the question. She uncrossed her arms and leaned her elbows on the table, leaning closer. "Did he go anywhere? Take you out of the car?"

I dropped my gaze to my hands in my lap and picked at that stray thread on my sleeve again. I didn't answer out loud, just shook my head no.

"So what happened?" She asked again.

I looked over to the mirror on the wall, trying to see through it at all, trying to see if Kip still stood behind the reflective surface.

"Hadley. What happened when he stopped at the rest stop?" She asked again, more forcefully.

I turned my head back around and looked her in the eye. "He raped me." I could hear the blood rushing through my ears and could feel the way my chest got painfully tight as I said the words out loud.

She didn't respond right away, just leaned back into her seat slightly. Tim dropped his hand off the table and gripped my good one on my lap, squeezing the hell out of it until l looked away from her to him.

He remained silent, but his eyes were sad as I looked back into them. A single tear dropped over my lower lid and slowly rolled down my face. I swallowed and unclenched my jaw a couple of times before looking back at her.

It surprised me to see compassion on her face. "I'm sorry, Hadley." She said softly before clearing her throat.

"He put the cloth over my mouth again and I blacked out. The next time I woke up we were at his house, and I had an IV line in my arm. He sedated me for the trip, I guess."

"What did he say or do when you got to his place?"

I held her stare as I went through the images in my head, "He put me in my grave." I said evenly and then took a couple of deep breaths, remembering how hard it'd been to breathe when I realized what he'd thrown me into. "He dug it before coming to New York and taking me. Said he'd wanted to make me dig it my-self, but that I probably would have used the shovel as a weapon against him. Because he could tell I'd fight back." I looked over to the mirror again, remembering

Kip's words when we'd first met, about how he didn't take me for the type of girl to just allow someone to beat on me. He'd been right. "I tried desperately to climb out of it, I clawed at the walls for hours trying to get out. I screamed until my voice broke."

"Where was the grave? Did he keep you in there the entire time you were there?" She asked as she motioned to the agent behind her. He quietly left the room as she continued to look at me, waiting for my reply.

"No. He took me inside when the sun rose again."

"What did he do when he took you inside?"

I couldn't do the back-and-forth all day. Not at that pace. I couldn't sit there and walk through six days, move by move of what he did to me. I'd die before I could finish.

As I locked eyes with her, I leaned forward, resting my arms on the table, and held her gaze as I explained. "I'm going to save you the trouble of acting like a parrot and asking me over and over what he did next. Throughout my time there, he consistently did the same thing every single day. He told me what a worthless, unwanted piece of trash I was. He told me repeatedly that when he was done with me, he'd rip the flesh from my bones and bury me in the grave he'd thrown me into numerous times. Then he beat me and tortured me with what-ever type of sick weapon he'd choose at that moment. You name it, he used it." I shrugged my shoulders and tried to act like it was nothing to say the words, when in reality it was everything. It took literally everything. "Whips, canes, knives, belts, baseball bats, plyers, or just his good ol' fists and boots. Those were his favorite because he said he could feel my flesh and bones bend-ing under them." Leaning back, I ran my hands through my hair, frustrated as I tried to find the right words. "He'd chain me up and keep me there for hours until he wanted to play again. Then he'd beat and torture me again until I lost consciousness, or he grew tired. Or in his particularly cruel moods, he would force me into whatever sick position he wanted, and he would rape me."

Kip would never want me after witnessing this. He was probably disgusted thinking about having me after that pig had forced himself inside of me.

My leg bounced uncontrollably under the table be-fore I stood up and started pacing. No one said anything as I moved around, my brain exploding with questions and answers. He'd never want me, and I couldn't even blame him. I felt like damaged goods, and they were forcing me to reveal just how damaged I was to the man I loved.

They all just watched me come unglued. My hands were clammy, and I started sweating, thinking about all the terrible things Peter Daniels did. I unzipped my jacket and took it off, folding it over the back of my chair, and tried to ignore the way they all looked when they saw the bruises, burns, and cuts still lingering on my arms.

I stopped in front of the mirror and instead of looking through it, trying to find Kip, I looked at myself in it, at what they were seeing on my skin.

More tears pooled in my eyes as I tried to come up with what to say next.

I stared at the tears in my eyes through the mirror until my vision blurred from them as I continued. "Eight times."

There was a quiet pause in the room, no one said anything right away until Agent Harvey spoke up. "What was eight times?" She asked. She stood up and walked over to the mirror and turned to face me, leaning her shoulder on it.

"He raped me eight times in six days." I turned my head to face her. "Don't think that because I paraphrased it for you that I don't remember what happened every single second of every day that he held me captive. I just can't sit here and talk about it step by step with you when you still think I'm lying about it." I said angrily.

Her right eye twitched again as she looked over at the others in the room before looking back at me.

"I'm trying here, Hadley. The crime scene looks bad for you, there's more evidence proving you murdered him than there is evidence to back up what you speak of. We didn't find any DNA from you in any room other than the living room where he was killed and in his car. We found the grave you talked about, but nothing else to support your claims. What else do you remember? Give me something solid."

I turned back and looked at Tim. He tried to hide it quickly as I turned, but I could read the grief on his face before he locked it down.

"He used a condom every single time he raped me because he said he didn't want to leave any traces of his DNA on me to lead the cops to him if they ever found my body." I paused again, looking back to Agent Harvey, "Because at that point, he was the monster, and I was the victim the police would be trying to get justice for.

But that was before I had to save myself." Taking another calming breath, I paused once more, attempting to gather my thoughts and speak coherently. "I remember every time he strangled me until I'd pass out when he wanted to move me without me fighting him. I remember the times he used the cane with a red handle on my kneecaps, he told me it was his favorite because the noise it made when it hit my bones made his dick hard." As my body trembled with anger and pain, I kept my gaze locked with hers. "I remember the burn of the shackles digging into the skin at my wrists and ankles when he'd chain me up and leave me for hours while he left. I remember begging God to kill me so that I could be free of his torment after he waterboarded me and then threw me down the stairs, only to pick me back up and take me to the top to throw me down them again."

It was evident that everyone was affected by what I said because there was a mixture of horror and pity on every face in the room. But I knew I needed to give them something they would know was the truth, undeniable proof. "But what I remember most is the way he nearly broke my back, shoving me into the closet next to the front door when Sheriff Boyd came to visit." I watched as all eyes turned to the Sheriff, but he remained oblivious to them because his gaze was fixed on mine, overwhelmed with absolute disbelief. My heart was breaking inside of my chest, I could physically feel the pain I'd felt in his home as I told them all what he did to me. The sheriff knew when I said I'd been there for six days that he had been there in that time frame. He had been trying to figure out how he could have missed the signs of Peter holding me against my will when he had been at the house.

So I talked to him directly as I went on. "You stopped by on my third day there. He'd just pulled me out of the ground where he'd made me stay overnight, naked and bleeding, for my disobedience in fighting him as he tried to rape me the last time. I was exhausted and suffering from hypothermia, so I was nearly unconscious when he started throwing me around. You pulled in as he shut the front door behind us and he panicked. He didn't have time to lock me back up or knock me out because you were getting out of your car and walking up the front walk. So he forced me into the closet and smashed my face in with his fist four times before telling me that if I made a sound, he would cut your throat open and hold me under it while you bled out all over me."

My body trembled as tears fell, "So I laid there in the closet, holding my hands over my mouth…" I shivered and my eyes fluttered closed as I cried, "praying for the strength to stay quiet while you spoke to that monster about the ice fishing derby going on that weekend and how you hoped the pike would be biting. I sobbed silently in the dark because I didn't want your death on my conscience when he finally killed me." I accused angrily, pointing my finger at him.

My chest shook as I tried to take a deep breath, but couldn't. I grabbed for the wall as my knees gave out and I fell to the floor in utter exhaustion. I brought my knees up and wrapped my arms around them as I laid my head back against the wall.

Tim rushed over and fell to his knees next to me, still silent.

I was so tired, I just wanted to crawl back into Kip's bed and hide from everyone. But I had to keep going. "The day he died is the day he tried to kill me for good. No more threats or attempts, he held the knife to my chest ready to plunge it in and get it over with. But I fought back. And when I fought back, I didn't stop fighting until I had stabbed him so many times I couldn't lift my arms anymore. I lived because he didn't." When every ounce of energy left my body all over again, I closed my eyes. "I grabbed what I could of my own things and left. He had no phone there that I could find, and I couldn't find the keys to his truck. So I grabbed my bag and ran into the blizzard to escape him for good. And it all would have been for nothing if Kip hadn't found me and saved me." I fought to keep my emotions in check as I got overwhelmed with my feelings for the lumberjack.

The alpha.

"The only reason I'm alive right now is because of him. He gave me a reason to fight to stay alive when, after everything, I was ready to just let death take me. I've gone from being the victim, to being the criminal, to being whatever it is that I've become now."

"You've become a survivor, Hadley." Tim said affectionately before looking up at the agent who just stood silently watching it all unfold, "That's enough, Agent. She's been through enough. You have everything you need."

"No, it's not enough," I said weakly. I found it hard to even lift my head off the wall.

"No, he's right, that's enough Hadley. We can clear you with your statement, assuming Sheriff Body here provides his statement about his visit to the house." She said, looking over to the older gentleman who easily nodded his head yes without question.

"No." I said, though. "That's enough of my story. But if I don't keep going, who's going to tell the stories of the other girls?"

Chapter 15 - Kip

While watching Hadley tell her story, so much anger filled me I almost broke the glass of the mirror and every other surface in the room multiple times. So much anger flowed through my body while watching her tell those sons of bitches what happened to her.

When she said that Boyd had been there while she was held captive and that she had forced herself to remain silent to save his life, I felt an immense sense of pride and an overwhelming love for her flooding over me. She had been incredibly brave and strong the entire time she was there and again while being questioned.

She was everything I'd convinced myself she wasn't. When I'd found her inside of my late kid's room, I thought her to be the most selfish person I'd ever met. That she couldn't even wait for me to tell her about them, and instead had forced my hand and found out herself. But instead of being selfish, she was the most caring person I'd ever met, living her life in selflessness every step of the way.

I hadn't been ready to unbox their memories from where I'd kept them locked up in my heart for so long, because that would mean they were really gone and that they were a part of my past, not my present or my future.

But I could see how it would be okay. They made me the man I had become when I was their father and Hadley was with me now that they weren't, to make me live true to what they'd made me, to hold me accountable and responsible for my actions. Which I'd tried doing after I realized I'd acted harshly and unjustly to her out of anger and pain. But by then she was slipping through my fingers as her own memories and past threatened to swallow her whole.

She didn't know it, but she had stopped directly in front of me on the other side of the mirror when she'd stared at her reflection, and having her so close yet so far from me and the protection of my arms, nearly killed me. I'd wanted to reach through the window and hold her and be her strength through it all.

Even if I was speculative about his relationship with her, I was glad she had Tim with her.

There was one thing I had learned during my brief time with Hadley.

To know her was to love her.

I knew he cherished her, even if it was just in an endearing friendship way. But I was glad for his friendship with her.

She collapsed to the floor after giving all she had left to give, and Tim called for it to be enough for today. I wanted to burst through the door and pick her up into my arms and carry her the entire way back to my house and take care of her.

But she stopped us all in our tracks.

"That's enough of my story. But if I don't keep going, who's going to tell the stories of the other girls?"

What?

Other girls?

The agent asked what we all wondered. "What are you talking about? What other girls?" Harvey said as she walked over closer and squatted down to be eye level with her like being closer would give her a better understanding.

Tim looked from her back to Hadley, trying to fig-ure it out too. My sweet bambina just opened her eyes slowly. "The other girls he kidnapped, raped, murdered, and buried. The girls from homeless shelters across the country where he *graciously* volunteered." She said bit-terly, "The other girls like me that had no one to report them missing or care if they were ever heard from again. The ones that had no one in the entire world to care. What about them?"

Harvey shook her head in disbelief as her mouth hung open, speechless as to what to say.

"You never found the cell, did you?" Hadley asked.

Harvey just shook her head in question again, still speechless.

Hadley's eyebrows pinched together in disbelief. "The room in the basement where he kept us. One at a time over the years. The one with the iron cell in the corner and all of the sick tools he used to torture us with. The one where he videoed all the pain he inflicted on us with a camera just like that one." She jutted her chin towards the camera mounted in the room's corner, recording her interrogation.

"We never found a basement entrance. W-we turned that place upside down." Harvey stuttered in disbelief. Sheriff Boyd stood up and walked closer as well.

"It's in the wall behind the bookshelf. Like in some mystery movie, the secret passageway in the bookshelf." Hadley said as she rolled her eyes at the memory. "He was so proud of his little secret lair beneath his home. He mocked me about entertaining church members and community leaders upstairs and breaking little girls downstairs."

"Will you show us?" Agent Harvey asked even though her face and tone gave away the fact that it was above and beyond what Hadley needed to do. They had already treated her like a prisoner and then interrogated her, forcing her to re-experience the hell she had survived.

"What?" Hadley gasped in astonishment.

I had heard enough; I needed to get to her. Leaving the room, ignoring the warnings of the agents in there with me, I opened the door to the interrogation room without knocking.

Everyone turned to look at me, not expecting someone to just barge in. But they obviously didn't know me or understand what I'd do for the scared and injured woman in the corner on the floor.

"Hell no, she won't go with you there," I answered for her as I maneuvered through the people milling around to get to my girl.

"I don't want to go back there, Kip." Hadley cried, looking up at me from the floor where she was still curled around herself, and I could see the fear in her fiery green eyes as tears still pooled in them. "They can't make me go back. Please." She begged hauntingly.

"You don't have to go back, baby. Not a chance in hell are you going back to that place." I squatted down in front of her, pulled her tiny body into my arms, and breathed her in. She clung to me like a lifeline and I reveled in having her in my arms again. She was safe in my arms.

"Hadley, I'd really like for you to reconsider. Beyond helping us get every piece of evidence that we obviously missed, it could be therapeutic for you to put it all to rest. Hadley, please reconsider. Putting it all to rest could be therapeutic for you, knowing that we discovered and told every single thing that happened to you at the hands of Peter Daniels - even validated it. It might help you heal." Agent Harvey prodded from behind me, her tone gentle but firm.

As Hadley pulled back from my arms, her gaze locked with mine, searching for something. I tried to relax my features when I saw the trepidation on hers. She searched my face for an answer, but I didn't want to make her do something one way or another. It had to be her decision.

"I need some air." She whispered to me. I nodded quickly before standing, helping her to her feet with my arms still wrapped around her.

"Where can she get some air that isn't crawling with the media?" I asked Boyd.

He turned and opened the door, motioning for us to follow him. "There's a courtyard out back that is surrounded by the building, it should be empty."

We didn't wait to ask the agent for permission as I led Hadley out under the bulk of my arm around her shoulders.

We stepped outside into the barren courtyard before I felt her take a deep breath again as the door shut behind us, leaving us in icy silence. The temperature was just above freezing, and Hadley wore only a short-sleeved shirt, so I shed my jacket and wrapped it around her as I pulled her into my chest, resting my chin on her head.

"How can you stand to touch me knowing everything now?" Her voice was so full of self-contempt, and I ground my teeth to quiet the scream that wanted to rip from my throat to the skies in agony.

Agony for her.

I leaned back and slid my fingers under her chin, physically forcing her head back to look up at me. She closed her eyes and her nostrils fluttered in time with her lips as she fought to keep her composure. Tears broke free from the corners of her eyes and her forehead wrinkled as she lost her hold on the pain.

As I slid my hands under her legs, lifting her up, her legs instinctively wrapped around my waist, and I walked towards a chair positioned next to an abandoned ashtray on the wall. I sat down and wrapped my arms around her tiny body and held her tight as she shook with sobs against my chest.

First, I kissed her hair and her forehead, then I slid my hands under the warmth of my jacket around her shoulders and let them feel the softness of her skin under her own shirt as I pulled her impossibly close.

"Because I love you, Hadley." I felt her body stiffen as I said those words to her, but I didn't pull away or let her shrink in on herself any more than she already was. "You are so incredible, and I love every single thing about you, including your scars baby. None of this changes that for me."

She tilted her head, and I felt her warm lips against my neck as she sniffled. "I don't understand how you're not repulsed by me," She leaned back and looked at me. "*I'm* repulsed by me!"

"Nothing changed from this morning to right now for me, except now I have the answers I so desperately wanted from you for weeks. But how I feel about you sexually hasn't changed. You didn't choose any of it, you didn't allow any of it to happen to you, Hadley. You're a survivor, and I'm so fucking proud to even be in your presence."

I leaned in and pressed my lips to hers, leaving the contact light because I could feel how on edge she was already, and I knew even though she was afraid I'd be repulsed by her body, she was raw from telling everyone of her horrors. And I didn't want to add to any pain.

She leaned her head to the side and deepened the kiss, letting her fingers tangle in the fabric of my shirt and pull me closer to her as my tongue pushed into her mouth.

I moaned when I tasted her for the first time all day and cupped the side of her face with my hand as I kissed her with everything I had.

I knew words were going to fall flat for a while with her, and that I had to use my actions to prove to her she was still desirable and still wanted by me.

"Do you mean it?" She asked, pulling back, and laying her forehead against mine, still keeping her eyes closed.

"Every word." I kissed her nose and took a deep breath, filling my lungs with her scent.

"Even the ones of love?"

I smiled and let her feel the smile on my lips as I pushed them to hers again, softly. "Especially those."

"What about everything that happened before Mike got there though, I still don't know what happened to your family and—"

I silenced her with a finger on her lips and she finally opened her eyes and looked into mine. "When you have room in your heart for that story, I'll tell you every single part of it. I don't want any more secrets or lies between us, baby. But I want to help you through this right now in any way that I can. We can talk about all of that later."

She took a deep breath, and I could see the fatigue in her muscles, even as she slid her palms flat against my stomach and chest and groaned when my body reacted the way it always did when she was in my arms.

"I'm sorry, I can't help it when you're touching me like this," I whispered to her lips before leaning in and taking a drink from them again.

She smiled against them before pulling back again.

I stayed silent and let her mind work out what it needed to in silent support.

"I think I have to go with them back to that prison. But I really don't know if I'm strong enough to." She whispered finally.

"If you let me, I'll be strong for you. I'll be right there with you the whole time, if that's what you want."

"I'm not sure if I want you to see it either, though. It would be unbearable if you saw everything and then—" She paused and shuddered, "didn't want me anymore. I wouldn't be able to stand it."

"That will not happen, baby. I'm in this. Headfirst. Unapologetically. Without reservation."

She looked me deep in the eyes and the outdoor lights made her eyes glow with golden fire as she tried to find the lie in my words, but there were none.

Finally, she just nodded her head and sighed, "Then I guess I'd rather just get it over with and then we can go back—" She broke off at the end.

"Home." I finished for her. "I want you to come back home with me."

"Are you sure?"

"Without reservation. Remember."

She leaned forward again and let her lips brush over mine softly, "I love you." She whispered. "I don't know why I had to endure such hell to find such peace with you, but I won't say I'm not glad to be where I am right now, regardless of how I got here."

"I could say the same exact thing, Hadley, the same fucking thing."

The door to the courtyard opened up and Boyd popped his head out, "Uh- sorry to interrupt, but we're getting ready to go if you'd like to go with us."

"Now or never Bambina."

Chapter 16 - Hadley

Breathe

I sat in the back of a police cruiser for the second time in the same day, but my hands were uncuffed and Kip held them in my lap from where he sat next to me. Police cars formed a convoy and headed towards the crime scene to carry out further investigations based on the information I had given them. I felt exhausted and sick just from driving towards the house I had escaped from.

When we pulled into the driveway, I took a deep breath and Kip squeezed my hands as I looked out the window at the modern house in the woods that had held me captive for six days.

I had to see it through.

I nodded to him curtly, granting him the permission he had been seeking. In response, he opened his door and extended a hand to help me out, while Sheriff Boyd,

Agent Harvey, and their team members also disembarked from their vehicles.

Agent Harvey walked up to me and looked me in the eye with respect instead of accusation like she had when she'd first walked into the interrogation room. Tim walked up behind her and lent his silent support as I prepared myself to rip open every wound that had just started to close.

She spoke up first, commanding the scene, "I have to ask that no one touch anything inside of the home, our crime scene team will touch anything that we need to with gloves so we can keep evidence accurate. Are you ready to lead us through there, Hadley?"

I swallowed and licked my dry lips as I looked over across the dark lawn to the spot where the flood lamps illuminated the grave I'd spent so much time in. A chill passed through my body, and Kip wrapped his arms around me and kissed my hair.

"He cannot hurt you anymore. I won't let him."

I smiled sadly up at him and then nodded my head and Agent Harvey led the way to the front door. She and Boyd walked in first, and we followed.

I instantly felt my body stiffen as I stepped over the threshold. We stood in the living room in silence for a moment as everyone looked around, seeing the space with fresh eyes since the truth came out.

Boyd couldn't tear his eyes away from the closet behind the door, and Harvey was staring longingly at the bookcase.

However, I couldn't look away from the crimson stain on the carpet in the middle of the room where I had taken the life of the man who had tortured me when he tried to permanently end my life.

I remembered the way the knife had slid in my hand as it plunged into his chest for the first time from the sweat on my palms.

I remembered the noises that escaped his throat as it violently leaked blood out onto us both as he struggled to breathe.

I remembered the smell of his life leaving his body.

Kip's body was coiled tight next to me and his grip on my hand was iron-tight as he fought his own emotions to be there with me. "Hey," I said, tearing my eyes away from the stain to look up at the man who had stolen my heart in such a short time. "You don't have to stay if it's too much for you. I'm sure this must bring back memories for you—"

"Stop." He commanded. "I'm irate because of what you went through here, not because of anything else. I'm here for you, and I'm not leaving."

"Okay." I loosened my hold on his hand and hated the way it felt empty as soon as it let go. Stepping around the yellow place markers outlining the stain, I walked towards the bookshelf and Agent Harvey as Kip reluctantly let me step out of his embrace. I stood next to her and pointed to the shelf halfway up on the end. "The screw on the outside board." I waited for her crime scene man to step forward and raise his glove-covered hand toward where I was talking about. I nodded when his hand touched the hole. "Push it in."

He did and there was a deafening click as the entire unit moved and he pulled it open, revealing a set of concrete stairs illuminated by an eerie green light dangling from a socket in the ceiling.

"Son of a bitch." Harvey said from next to me as she looked to the stairway. She drew her gun and motioned for me to stay back as she and her team slowly descended the stairs and cleared the room below. "It's empty." She yelled back up and beckoned for me to come down.

Kip slid his hand along the small of my back and I leaned into him. "My brain is trying to tell me he's down there waiting for me. Which I know is crazy, but—" I couldn't tear my eyes away from the rough stairs that had inflicted so much pain on my body each time he threw me down them.

"I'll go first," Kip said, waiting for me to look at him. "Remember what I said. I'm never going to let anyone hurt you ever again."

He walked down the steps and turned to look at me halfway down and then walked down the rest of them, looking around the room before calling back for me. "Come on down, baby."

Tim walked up next to me and took a deep breath, "That man has it bad for you, Hadley."

I was surprised when I actually chuckled and nudged his arm with my shoulder. "I'd be lost without him."

I took the last step towards the stairs and Kip stood at the bottom, looking up at me and holding his hand out for me, so I forced my feet to take the steps down until my hand slid into his.

The smell hit me first and instantly sucked me back into the darkness of the iron cell in the damp basement air.

The tiny cell sat in the corner and his workshop of torture devices lined the walls. I leaned into Kip's side as he looked around and saw everything that had left distinct marks on my body.

I watched as the agents took pictures of everything, looks of pure shock and disgust covered their faces as they finally saw their victim for the monster that he was.

The red-handled cane stole my gaze and wouldn't let go. So much pain. Fuck, it had caused devastating agony across my body with each swing.

"Breathe, Hadley," Kip whispered into my ear and held me.

But if I took a deep breath, I'd remember the fear I'd felt while sitting in the pitch black alone in the cell, unsure if it was day or night. Unsure if that would be my last day on Earth, or if he'd keep me alive for more torture.

I couldn't breathe down there.

"He kept the video files over there." I pointed at the wall that had a bunch of storage bins labeled with dates and names on them.

Agent Harvey walked over and quickly opened one with her gloved hands and looked back at me, shocked. She turned around again and looked at the many bins.

"There has to be fifty different labels on these. Fifty different girls?"

"At least," I answered and took a gargled breath as my lungs ached for air. "He talked about how he'd been doing it for decades." More memories assaulted me. I could hear his voice.

"My God." She whispered as she stepped back so her team could photograph them. "Where are the bodies buried? Did he tell you?"

I shook my head and shrugged my shoulders. My mind was screaming in agony and my heart was splintering further the longer I was down in the basement. I needed fresh air; I couldn't take a deep breath.

I could smell his skin.

"In the woods, he didn't say where exactly."

I could see the emptiness in his eyes.

I could feel the squeezing of his hands around my neck.

"Kip-," I gasped, my voice cutting out. My skin was tight on my arms and hands. I felt an icy shiver run down my spine and tingles break out over my body.

"Hadley?" Kip called, putting his hands on each side of my face and making me look at him. "What's wrong?"

But I couldn't see him past my memories. I couldn't see anything.

You're my favorite trophy yet. My most prized possession. You feel so good.

My mind swarmed as I tried desperately to keep the past and the present separate. My eyes wouldn't focus on anything as noises sounded far away suddenly.

"Baby, look at me. Look right into my eyes." Kip was crouched down in front of me, trying desperately to get my eyes to look at him. My chest felt like the monster was sitting on it again.

"I can't breathe," I whispered, forcing the words through my dry throat. "Help me." I felt the panic rise in my nerves as I clutched at my throat. "Please, help me," I begged as Kip's hands ripped mine from my throat where I was digging at the skin with my nails, desperate to release the hold the ghost had on me.

"We're done. I'm getting her the fuck out of here." Kip barked as he slid his arms under my legs and picked me up. He ran up the stairs as I buried my face in his neck. "I'm right here Had. Feel me. Smell me. You're safe. I'm with you."

I held my breath as darkness descended over my vision completely, my arms clinging to Kip like a buoy in the middle of the ocean of turmoil.

When we made it outside, a rush of fresh air snapped against my skin, making me gasp as I drew it into my lungs, soothing the burning ache inside of them.

"That's it. Take a deep breath." He said as he sat me down in the front seat of Tim's rental truck. He turned my body, so my legs were hanging off the seat out the door and he stepped in between them and hugged me to his body like he was my life raft. Holding onto him tightly, I surrendered to his scent enveloping me, bringing calm to my pounding heart and chaotic mind.

As soon as I regained the ability to form a coherent sentence, I weakly uttered into his neck. "I don't want to be here anymore."

"Then we'll leave." He barked orders around to people who had come out of the house after us and before I knew it, I was being whisked away into the back seat of the truck and tucked into his lap as Tim drove us back to Kip's house.

I kept my eyes closed and my mind focused on his chest rising and falling under my cheek and timed my own to his and before I knew it, I was drifting into a dazed sleep. Worn out and drained, he lifted me from the truck, saying something to Tim, and then walked us into his home.

When we walked in, I was vaguely aware that Mike was sitting in the living room with Dev, but I didn't pay attention to what they said as Kip carried me upstairs to his bedroom.

He stripped me out of my clothes and pulled a long-sleeved shirt of his over my head before sliding his bare body in next to mine under the heavy weight of the blankets.

"You are so unbelievably strong." He whispered into my hair. "I love you so fucking much Hadley."

My body succumbed to exhaustion, and as sleep enveloped me like a menacing creature lurking in the depths of dark water, I answered back. "I love you too."

Praying for a reprieve from the chaos in my mind, I went willingly.

Chapter 17 - Kip

Home

She'd nearly passed out in that fucking basement. Her eyes had glassed over, and her pupils dilated as she went basically unresponsive.

Kip. Help me. Please, help me.

Her words ignited a fire in my soul that would never burn out again.

She needed me to protect her and help her, and that's exactly what I planned to do for as long as she allowed me to be in her life. Which I hoped to be for a very long fucking time.

I loved her.

Holding the tiny breathtaking woman in my arms in my bed after everything she endured made me realize I was fucking done.

Stick a fork in me, I was done, never to be the same again.

Her breath warmed the skin on my neck with each breath as I laid there and continued to hold her long into the night. But sleep wouldn't take me under.

I replayed the events of the day back through my head over and over endlessly. I had no idea how she stayed on her feet as long as she had after the emotional turmoil I'd put her through before any of the police bullshit even started.

When I'd stripped her bare for bed, there was a new bruise on her shoulder and my blood boiled when I'd realized I'd done that to her in my haste to get her out of my kids' room.

I was no better than Peter Daniels. I marked her with physical force, even if it was an accident, and yet she still loved me.

Well, never again. I'd never allow myself to become so overcome with grief and shame again that I'd touch her physically like that. Never.

I didn't deserve the angel in my bed. But I was damn sure going to work on earning the right to have her in my life every minute forward.

I looked over her shoulder at the clock on the end table. It was nearly three am, and we'd climbed into bed after midnight. She was so peaceful in my arms, and I could feel some of that peace settle into my body through our contact.

Eventually, I fell asleep, pulling her tighter into my arms and trying to absorb as much of her into my soul as possible.

I dreamt of her.

Her touch made me feel warm and happy, and my body responded physically as she showed me how much she adored me with her touch. Her lips kissed their way down my chest and stomach, and then she nipped the skin of my hips with her sharp teeth before soothing it with her tongue.

Her breath was warm, and she chuckled when I jerked my hips forward, desperate for more of her touch.

"Always wanting more." She whispered before tasting the tip of my cock with her tongue.

"Fuck." I moaned as her wet tongue licked my cock from base to tip and then twirled over the head before she swallowed it deep into her mouth, pressing the back of her throat down on it and gagging. She pulled off and licked back up it before doing it again, taking more of me deeper into her throat before she pulled off.

What a fucking dream. Before I opened my eyes, I groaned and stretched, waking up and getting lost in the moment for a minute. I looked over to her side of the bed and that was when I realized it was empty and I hadn't been dreaming at all.

Because laying between my thighs looking up at me through her dark eyelashes as she swallowed my cock was the most beautiful woman in the world and I groaned and pushed my hips forward, seeking more from her wet mouth.

"Fuck." I groaned and tangled my fingers in her hair. "How do you make that feel so fucking good?" I asked. I was panting as she worked me with her mouth and both tiny hands. She chased her mouth with her tight fists and hummed when I was deep in her throat, working me deeper. And then my sleep and lust-filled brain caught up and remembered what happened yesterday. "Stop, we don't have to do this, Hadley. Not after-"

"Give me this. Please." She said with a calm seriousness in her eyes. "I need your touch to cover the memories of that house. I need you to wash it all away."

Her swollen lips kissed the base of my cock when she finally worked me completely down her throat and I groaned as the urge to pump her stomach full of my come was nearly overcoming my senses.

"I want to do this right for you, but I also want to blow down your throat so fucking bad," I said, as she eagerly bobbed her mouth up and down, daring me to do just that. Never in my life had I experienced a woman who could actually deep-throat my entire cock, given its size. It was fucking heaven.

She pulled off and dropped her mouth to my balls and teased them with her tongue before dropping lower and licking my taint.

"Shit!" I cursed as her tiny tongue pushed on a hot button under the skin while her hands fisted my cock, drawing my orgasm closer to the surface.

I reached down and pulled her up my body until she straddled my waist, and I buried my tongue in her mouth and kissed her soul.

"I have a much better place for you to blow." She purred against my lips and grabbed my cock between us, rubbing the head of it through her soaking wet lips before sinking down and taking the head of it into her hot pussy.

"Do you?" I asked, grinding my teeth to keep my hips still while she played with me, pleasing herself on my cock.

"Yes." She moaned as I leaned in and sucked her nipple into my mouth and then bit it.

"Tell me where you want my come." I demanded as my hips jerked and impaled her further onto my cock, unable to stand her slow torture anymore.

She pulled back and buried her fingers in my hair and pulled it, drawing another groan from my lips as she sunk completely onto my cock. "I want you to fill my pussy up. I want your come dripping out of my body all fucking day long."

I laid back on the bed and lifted her, raising her up over my cock. Then I slammed my hips forward to fill her with it again before dropping back to the bed and doing it again. "Your wish is my command, angel."

I fucked her like a crazed man, she put her hands on my chest and dug her nails into my pecks as I filled her body over and over with my cock. She moaned and circled her hips with each thrust, throwing her head back and holding on as she took every pounding. Her tits bobbed with each punishing thrust and she was my biggest fantasy come to life.

"You look like a fucking angel taking my cock like this. God, you do insane fucking things to me when you let me take you like this." I pushed my heels into the bed and lifted with more force, reveling in the gasp that left her lips each time my pubic bone smashed into her clit.

"I'm going to—" she gasped and bit her lip, moaning as she rocked her hips again. "Don't stop, you're making me come. Oh, my god, I'm coming so hard, Kip!" She yelled and her pussy clenched down tightly on my cock as she milked it, demanding my come.

And I gave into her need and roared as the first shot of come erupted out of my cock and deep into her pussy. She screamed and her back bowed as her orgasm ripped her body apart. "Kip!" She moaned and rocked her hips back and forth as she continued to come.

I stilled and watched with fascination as she rubbed her clit on my pelvis over and over and moaned. I felt her body shoot off again, clenching down on my cock as her orgasm tried pulling more into her body.

"You greedy girl." I teased and flipped her onto her back, pushing her legs wide and bringing her knees to her sides and ground down on her clit with my body, while my cock continued to stroke leisurely in and out of her sinful body.

"I can't stop- please don't stop, I want more." She leaned up and bit my neck, her tiny teeth breaking through the skin as she moaned repeatedly.

"Fuck!" It felt so fucking good to have her so unraveled underneath me, and before I knew it, I was pounding my cock into her body again. I never went soft thanks to her overwhelming tightness and the wetness of our mutual orgasms made her pussy so fucking silky and wet. "I can't stop fucking you even if I wanted to, Hadley. You drive me absolutely insane with the need to fill you."

I was toeing the line of having a full-on breeding kink breakthrough with the fucking minx and barely held back all the dirty things I ached to tell her.

I wanted to breed her so fucking badly. Luckily she was on birth control, so I didn't let lust cloud my better judgment in the moment, but the act of giving her my DNA and come was enough for the time being.

"I need to be filled. I've never let a man come inside of me before you, and now it's all I can think about. You make me crave your come like it's my favorite drug."

"Do you have any idea what those dirty words on your pretty fucking lips do to me?" I asked, reaching between us to pinch her nipple and bury my tongue in her mouth when she opened it to cry out. I absorbed her scream and pushed her body over the edge again as she exploded under me again. Her whole body convulsed as she clawed at me, desperately trying to pull me even deeper. "That's a good girl. Fucking take what I give you."

Her eyes rolled as my own dirty talk spurred her on.

"You love letting me use your body, don't you?"

"Yes!" She begged. "I can't believe I've come so many times; I come so fucking hard with you buried deep inside of me. You fuck me so good."

"I was made to fill you with my cock and come. No one else has ever felt so fucking good."

She threw her head back again and bit her lip. I slammed my body into hers, giving her everything I had left in me, and roared as my balls shot electricity through my body and started filling her again. My entire body cramped up as I felt my come dripping out of her tight body around my cock and I pulled out and knelt between her legs as I gasped for my breath.

She had her hands in her hair as she, too, gasped over and over. She opened her eyes and looked at me with such wonder and shock in her gaze.

I dropped my eyes to her pink pussy and pushed her knees back even further, opening her to my eyes, and groaned when I saw the opaque evidence of my two orgasms dripping from her pussy and down over her tiny ass hole.

I let go of one knee and ran my fingers down through the wetness, rubbed it over her lower lips, and marked her with my come. She moaned and watched my eyes with rapture as I explored. I let my fingers fall further and rubbed my come over her ass, letting the silky lubrication of it work against her right entrance.

"Have you ever been fucked in the ass before?" She gasped and bit her lip, shaking her head no. "Have you ever taken anything in here?"

"No." She moaned.

"You've never let anyone play with your ass before, yet you're letting me?"

"I'm not letting you, Kip. I'm begging you." She said, panting as she reached down and grabbed both breasts in her hands and played with her nipples. "You make me wild with desire."

"I can't wait to push my cock into here someday. I can't wait to see your tight ass swallow my entire cock until I'm balls deep inside of it." While still stroking her entrance with my fingers, I revealed everything I desired to do to her lush body for her pleasure.

She closed her eyes, moaning, and arched her back, putting pressure against my fingers.

"Hold your knees wide open for me, baby," I commanded, and she grabbed them and pulled them wide for me. "Good girl. Fuck, you're such a good girl."

She loved being praised. I had noticed it the few times I had praised her before, but after learning about how her self-esteem had been beaten out of her throughout her life, it made perfect sense. She craved it because it made her feel wanted and deserving. She was never anything less to me, but I would give her what she needed so she'd believe it, too.

I pressed my middle finger against her ass and pushed the tip past the tight ring of muscles until my entire first knuckle was in her ass.

She gasped and held her breath as I invaded her virgin hole. "Tell me how that feels for you."

"It burns." She licked her lips and rotated her hips, "It feels good, though." She paused and looked at me. "Like I've been empty before and now I want to be filled."

I closed my eyes and hung my head as her words did dark and dirty things to my soul. "You're so fucking perfect for me, baby." I leaned over her body and kissed her lips, letting my tongue tangle with hers as she rubbed her pussy against my stomach, rubbing the wetness into my skin and pleasing her clit. I chuckled against her lips and pulled my finger from her ass before gathering more come on it and pushed it back in, quicker this time.

She moaned and let go of her knees to dig her nails into my arms as she held on and rode the ride I was putting her body through.

I leaned up far enough to push the fingers of my other hand against her clit and rubbed it hard as I worked my finger in and out of her ass. I pushed in until the second knuckle of my finger breached her entrance.

She gasped and writhed under me, "Your finger feels so big. Your cock will never fit in my ass, it's too big. You're too big."

"I'm going to stretch you with my cock before you even realize you're ready for it. And you're going to beg me to fuck you harder and deeper the entire fucking time."

She grabbed my cock where it was growing once again between us. She fisted it and stroked it against her belly as she climbed closer to her orgasm again. "I want your come to cover my skin."

I growled and mashed my teeth together again. "You don't realize what you're asking of me, baby. I've already come twice." But my cock burned with her words and her fists, even if my mind told me there was no way. "I'm an old man compared to you, sweetheart. I'm shocked I came twice as quickly as I did already."

"I need to feel you in me and on me at the same time. I need it so badly, Kip. You make me unequivocally crazy with need."

My hips thrust forward, pushing my cock through her hand faster. "Squeeze tighter," I growled against her lips. Her tiny fists squeezed around my thick cock, and she bit her lip as I picked up the pace in her ass. "Bare down, push more of my come out of your pussy and down onto my finger."

Her eyes rolled at my words, but she did just that, I felt her pussy and ass tighten and then more warm liquid coated my finger, slickening it up even more as I pushed it in deep in her ass, filling her completely with it. "Fuck, that burns." She groaned.

"Good girl. I'm fucking your virgin ass with my finger, getting it ready for my cock. Tell me you want my cock in here."

"God yes! I can't wait to feel you fuck my ass with your cock. You'll be the only man ever to have such a gift. I'll never let another man take me there."

Her words burned her brand into my alpha, and I fought the urge to climax again. "Holy shit, what you do to me with those words."

I used my other hand to push two fingers deep into her wet pussy and she mewed and moaned, struggling under me as I filled her in both holes without warning.

"Look at your pretty little body, so full of me," I said, looking down at where I worked her pussy and her ass together.

Her hands started stroking my cock faster, and she begged me to give her what she wanted. "I need you to come, Kip. I need you to fucking cover me with it."

"Good girl. Just like that, stroke me just like that." Bowing my head, I forced my jaw to loosen. "I'll come all over your tits and stomach as soon as you come on my fingers. I want to feel your virgin ass milk my fingers with your—"

I didn't get another word out because her ass and pussy did just what I told them to do. They clamped down on my fingers simultaneously and she screamed into the rafters and started thrashing under me. It was all I needed.

I didn't think it was possible, but hot spurts of come shot from my cock and branded her skin, covering every inch from her nipples to her clit as she continued stroking me. She aimed my cock as I covered her skin, just how she wanted.

"Holy fuck." She moaned, her hands stilling on me and then going limp at her sides when she could no longer hold them up off the bed.

I slowly slid my hands from her body and collapsed next to her, letting her lower her legs for the first time in forever. She groaned, and I rolled over to kiss her face over and over again as we both came back to earth.

We looked down her body and her lips curled up in a smile as she brought her dainty finger down to a pool of come on her tit and dipped it in it before bringing it to her lips.

She sucked her finger into her mouth and her eyes fluttered closed as she moaned. "You taste so good."

I pulled her lips to mine and shoved my tongue into her mouth. When I finally pulled back, I smiled against her bruised lips, "Hmm, so do you."

She chuckled and then sighed. "I need a shower. You got me all dirty." She joked, trying to keep a straight face.

"You begged me to make you dirty."

"Yes, I did." She leaned over and kissed me before gently sliding from the bed on sore muscles.

Her body was healing from her attack, but I still felt a wave of regret for handling her so roughly and for such a long time.

"I'm sorry—" I started, from where I sat up in bed.

She spun on me and pointed her finger at me. "Don't you dare!" I stopped in my tracks, and she leveled me with a very commanding glare. "I begged for every single thing you did to me, and every fucking thing gave to me. I don't regret one second of it, so don't you dare try to."

"How did you know what I was going to say?"

She raised her eyebrow at me and then turned to walk down the stairs in her naked beauty. I jumped from bed and gave chase as she called over her shoulder. "Because believe it or not, I'm starting to know you inside and out."

"Hmm." I hummed as I plastered my chest to her back and walked down the hall to the bathroom pressed against her body. "I don't know if I like that or not."

She chuckled as I stepped around her, turned the water on in the shower, and let it come to temp as I leaned down and kissed her neck. I could feel my come on her skin as I pressed myself against her and groaned. "My balls are so fucking empty from filling you up, yet I still want to fuck you more."

"Good. Because I'm far from being satisfied in my thirst for you." She purred seductively and then stepped into the hot water and looked over her shoulder at me, beckoning me to join her.

I couldn't let her get lonely, now could I?

We went back to sleep after our early morning sex, and she woke up long after her usual sunrise time and I knew it was because of the exhaustion she felt both physically and emotionally after the events in town.

But I needed to take her back to the police station to complete her statement with the FBI. I checked the news quietly before she woke up and the story was all over every single channel.

Small town Pastor? Or a long-time serial Killer?

Utah Pastor traveled to inner cities all over the nation, targeting and murdering at-risk women.

Saint turned to Demon. How did no one know what one pastor did on his frequent trips across the country to volunteer with America's at-risk youth?

Hadley Shaw. Once a suspect, now a survivor in the case heard around the world.

The headlines were all different, but the story was the same; Hadley was a survivor and a victim, not the suspect anymore. She had her name cleared, but the stares and shock from the small-town Utah residents would take a while to wear off if she went out in public.

I needed to help her through it because she deserved to walk down the street and hold her head high as we lived out our lives in my hometown.

If she asked me to move, however, I would in a second. But I'd be leaving behind every last piece of my family to do so. They buried Molly and my kids in town in the same cemetery where all of my ancestors were buried. The cabin was the place we brought them to on vacation. The locals were the people who remembered them with me.

Only time would tell what she wanted to do, but we'd do it together. Because I was deeply committed to her. I was invested in her.

Chapter 18 - Hadley

I sat in the armchair by the fireplace that I had taken as my own, inside of Kip's home. He was brewing a pot of coffee and walking around in a pair of low-slung sweatpants, and nothing else as he set up our cups perfectly. He was hovering and if he were anyone else, he'd be smothering, but with him it was perfect and I craved his attention for the time being.

As he poured our cups, the rich scent of coffee wafted through the room. He walked over to me, his steps soft on the floor, and leaned down to give me a sweet morning kiss. After handing me my coffee, he joined me on the couch, his presence warm and comforting.

He'd been perfect last night, giving me everything I needed from him as I tried to find a balance sexually between trauma and healing. We'd laid up for hours after our multiple rounds and talked and I told him how

I felt shame at finding pleasure in sex with him because of my torture by Peter Daniels.

Saying the words out loud had been so therapeutic as we worked through my feelings on it all until we fell asleep again and slept in until midafternoon. He didn't go outside to see to chores or responsibilities, and instead pulled on a pair of sweats and slippers and hovered right within reach.

"I love you," I said, taking another sip of my coffee and smiling behind my cup as the darkness fell from his face and joy took its place.

"I love you too, Had." He said easily, reaching over and taking my almost healed hand in his and rubbing his fingers over the closed wounds on the back of it. "We have to go into town today to sign your statement." He said, and I watched the darkness descend back over his features as he fought with that information.

"I know," I said calmly. "You don't have to go if you don't want to."

His eyes snapped up to mine, and his scowl deepened. "I'm going." He growled. "Knock that off."

I raised my eyebrows at him but stayed silent, almost smiling at his alpha peeking through. He sighed and set his cup down on the coffee table and then reached over, picking me up and setting me down in his lap and taking a deep breath.

"I just want to do this right, Hadley. I want to protect you and shelter you from the stares and whispers that I know are going to come your way from well-meaning but nosey people in town. And then there's the fact that this is a national story, so I know there are people who are going to come from far and wide to see everything firsthand, and I hate it. I just want to keep you here, safe and protected from it all."

"I know, baby," I said, laying my head on his shoulder and relaxing into his touch. "But if I'm going to live here with you from now on, we need to rip the band-aid off and let them stare so that hopefully they get over it sooner rather than later."

He looked down at me, "You want to live here, with me?"

I sat up and scowled at him, "Do you not want me to?"

"No!" He said quickly before rolling his eyes, "I mean yes, I want you here, I just didn't know if you'd want to stay or if you'd want to move somewhere else far away from everything that happened here. Like maybe Florida."

"I want to be here with you, Kip. I want to spend my days like this with you and Dev and forget the rest of the world exists outside of the trees surrounding us."

"I am a big fan of that idea." He said, relaxing on the couch and tightening his arms around my hips. We sat in silence for a while, watching the scenes of nature play out through the giant windows until he finally broke the stretch.

"My son Dalton was six, and my daughter Daisy was almost five." His deep voice was soft, and I could hear the pain in it as I silently sat in his lap and prayed my heart wouldn't beat out of my chest as he ripped his open to share his life with me. "I was on my ninth month of a tour in the Middle East when I got an emergency call from Mike." He took a shuddering breath, and I leaned my head back to look at him. "Two men broke into our home in town, in the middle of the night. When the kids didn't show up for school the next morning, Molly's sister went over to check on them." His entire body trembled with both violence and grief as he stared out the window. "They were all shot in their beds where they lay, asleep. They never had a chance of escaping."

"I'm so sorry, Kip," I said, shaking my head as tears stung my eyes. "Did they catch the men that did it?"

He sighed and tightened his arms around my waist and finally looked over at me. "Yeah, one of their girlfriends caught him cheating a few days later and turned him in to the police for revenge." He scoffed.

"I'm so sorry you had to go through that, and I'm so sorry for them, too."

"I'm sorry I didn't tell you sooner, I just… haven't dealt with it yet and I struggled with feeling like I was cheating on Molly with you, and in turn, I felt like I was being disloyal to you in the same. It's hard to wrap my head around it all."

"We have nothing but time," I said, running my fingers down through his beard as he took a deep breath and relaxed in my arms. "Nothing else is guaranteed in life, especially for us, but right now, we have nothing but time to figure it all out."

Epilogue – Kip

I set the ax on the ground and leaned on the handle as I stared up at the house, awestruck at usual. Hadley stood on the new wrap-around porch, reaching up above her head with a cute little pink watering can to water the hanging basket I bought her last week.

She wore a red sundress that hugged her lush curves in ways that made my mouth water with need. I had been obsessed with her since the moment I laid eyes on her two years ago, but my hunger for her only grew more each day since her body started changing to accommodate the growth of our first child.

And by the looks of it, I'd be keeping her barefoot and pregnant for many, many years to come. Pregnancy fucking suited her.

Which suited me just fine, because those thoughts I'd had in the very beginning, leading me to think I had a breeding kink, were accurate. I sure fucking did.

I had a *Must Breed Hadley Kink*. Somehow, she held me off for almost two years before she gave in and let me put my baby inside of her. But now that I did, I wasn't going to stop.

And even if she was already six months pregnant, I was going to see if I could possibly get her more pregnant. Luckily for me, her pregnancy hormones had translated into an insatiable sex drive and she rode my cock every chance she got over the last few months.

I dropped the ax on the ground and pulled my gloves off, tossing them onto my chopping block before I started the hike up the hill to the house. The warm July air allowed me to work in less clothing, so I had less to strip off on my way to my beautiful wife.

She spotted me at the bottom of the stairs and giggled when I toed off my boots on the ground and then my socks, leaving them in a pile as I sauntered up the steps.

"Mr. Montgomery," She set the watering can down and put her hands on her hips, "Your chores are nowhere close to being done for the day."

I grinned at her silently as I pulled my belt open and then undid my jeans, drawing her eyes down my abs and to my waist on my way to her.

"Kip," She hummed, cocking her head to the side as I pulled down my zipper and stood in front of her.

"Hadley," I growled back and fingered the tie holding the front of her dress closed over her juicy tits.

"It's only three in the afternoon." She batted my hand away playfully as I pulled the tie free, revealing the sexy swell of her breasts beneath the fabric. She didn't wear a bra when we were home alone because her hormones had made them grow so large she hated how restricting it felt. And I sure as fuck would not complain about my sexy wife letting me see the sensual swaying of them and her hard nipple peaks through her clothing every day. "You said this morning you had a full day of things to do."

"I do." I slid one button free beneath the tie and revealed more of her beautiful chest to my eyes as she put her hands back on her hips, but didn't stop me. "And right now, you're the next thing on my to-do list, baby." I pulled another button free until her pretty dress hung open above her round belly.

She giggled and tipped her head back when I leaned forward and kissed her neck, undoing the rest of her buttons until her dress opened down the front completely. I pushed it off her body as she swung her arms around the back of my neck, leaning into me as my hands danced down her back and cupped her ass. "Kip," She moaned gently when her hard nipples brushed against my bare stomach. "Mike and Darla invited us for dinner at their place later, you know that."

"That's three hours away," I sucked on her neck and brought my hands up between us to cup her juicy breasts, flicking her nipples with my thumbs and making her moan deeply. "You give me more credit than I'm due, baby. I'll fuck you so good and still have two hours and fifty minutes left to spare."

She giggled and pulled my head away from her neck with a handful of my hair and kissed me. I backed us up to the large outdoor daybed she loved on the porch, and sank down onto it, pulling her with me until she straddled me. I leaned back against the cushions and thrust my hips up against her panty covered pussy as she rocked side to side to get comfortable in my lap.

"I can never say no to you." She sighed, running her nails over my neck as I palmed both of her breasts, playing with them like an adolescent teenager, feeling his first pair of tits. I'd never bore of them, and the fact that she could come from nipple stimulation alone these days, just added to the fun. "Mmh, more of that."

She shimmied her tits in my hands and pulled my face forward to them.

"Beg me so nicely." I teased, licking my lips and eyeing up her nipples, already aching to taste them, but hesitating just enough to toy with her.

"Please, baby." She moaned, rocking herself against my jean covered cock, "I know you want to play with them."

"Mmh." I growled, leaning forward to suck one into my mouth. "They're my favorite toys." She giggled and then tipped her head back as I feasted on her sensitive nipples. She rocked her hips back and forth, teasing us both as I sucked, nibbled, and licked her repeatedly. "Take my cock out, baby."

She deftly reached under her body and pulled my cock out as I shimmied out of my jeans and kicked them onto the porch.

"Now what?" She purred seductively, running her thumb back and forth over the tip, playing with the pre-cum that leaked out.

"Now," I grabbed the waistband of her panties and pulled, ripping them apart and tossing them onto the porch behind her, "slowly sink down onto it and come while I suck on these pretty fucking tits."

She gasped and leaned up far enough to spit in her palm and stroke my cock with it, coating me before lining it up and slowly sinking down onto it. She was still as tight as the first time I sank into her and I fought the urge to thrust up, forcing her to take me completely.

"God, I love your cock." She mewled and sank down onto me, digging her nails into my shoulders and pulling me tighter against her chest. "Just like that." She rocked on my cock and rubbed her clit against my pelvis, pleasuring herself like I was her personal toy to be used. And I absolutely loved when she did that. "Harder, suck them harder, Kip."

I did as she demanded and she cried out, lifting herself up and then slamming back down into my lap.

"Fuck!" She cried, tightening down onto my cock and spasming as she orgasmed. "Yes!" Her scream echoed off the surrounding trees, and I used my grip on her hips to keep her moving long after she lost the rhythm to her pleasure. When she sank forward in release, I gently lifted her and turned us so she was lying on her back on the bed. Her pretty dark hair fanned out and the orgasmic blush covered her chest and face as she smiled up at me. "Come here." She pulled me forward to reenter her, but I had other plans, dodging her grasp and spreading her thighs wide as I sank to my knees between them. "Oh."

I chuckled, blowing on her swollen clit and flicking my tongue across it. Her tits were my first choice to play with, her pussy was a close second. I often woke her up, with my head buried between her thick thighs, and wouldn't fuck her until she came multiple times.

It was insane how attracted I was to my wife, in a deep, animalistic way that consumed me day and night.

"I need you to come on my face." Growling, I sucked on her clit, pushing my fingers into her pussy. "I fucking *need* it, Hadley."

She stretched out under me like a cat waking up from a sunny afternoon nap, pushing her clit against my tongue harder. "Whatever you want." She smiled and buried her fingers in my hair around the growing swell of her baby belly.

I didn't drag it out, because the noises she made left me aching to bury myself back into her warm body like a dying man reaching for his life as it slipped through his fingers. She was my heaven, my peace, and my place of rest. I had never experienced true peace like I found in Hadley's arms and body.

"That's it," She cried out, arching into me as I curled my fingers inside of her and sucked hard on her clit. She unraveled, crying my name as she started trembling as her orgasm shattered inside of her. "God, baby." She collapsed into the cushions when I pulled back and sat on my heels between her spread thighs.

"Do you want to stop?" I asked, rubbing the fatigued muscles in her legs. As bad as I wanted to rut into her like an animal, I knew she had limits that grew every day she progressed in her pregnancy.

Hadley scoffed, lifting one leg and swinging it over in front of me to get to her knees. She glanced seductively over her shoulder as she knelt in front of me. She pushed her knees wide and dropped her chest to the bed, lifting her round ass further into the air.

"Fuck me, Kip. I want you to show me just how badly you still need me."

I spanked her ass cheek, sending the cracking noise echoing through the forest around us, followed by her excited shriek as I lined my cock up with her dripping hole. I gave her just the head of my cock, teasing her as I shook her large ass cheeks, making them ripple seductively.

Doggy was her new favorite position because she didn't feel smothered by the pressure of the baby on top of her, and I wasn't complaining when I had the erotic sight of her ass in my lap to stare at as I fucked her.

She let me tease her for a few thrusts, playing along with my game until she couldn't take it any longer. She threw her ass back on my next thrust, impaling herself on my entire cock, moaning out and doing it again.

"My sexy little minx," I growled, spanking her ass as she twerked it up and down on my cock. "I fucking love your needy side."

"I'm always needy," She panted, reaching underneath her to roll her clit beneath her fingertips as I slammed in deep, fucking her how she wanted.

"Mmh," I hummed, reaching around her body and pulling her up by her shoulders to sit back in my lap and then turned us to face the windows of the house behind the daybed. Our reflection was crystal clear as I grabbed a handful of her hair, pulling her head to the side and thrusting into her from below. She sagged into my touch and palmed both of her breasts as I fucked her. As I teased her clit, she arched her back and gripped the back of my neck, leaning into me for support and allowing me to pleasure her. "You're a fucking goddess," I strummed her clit in time with my thrusts and stared at her in the window. "Look at you taking me so perfectly."

She opened her eyes and shivered as she stared at us, moving in rhythm and ecstasy. "You make me feel so sensual and beautiful." She hummed, pinching her nipple and moaning. "Even as my body changes, you make me feel cherished and desired."

"Because you are," I growled, fucking her harder. "I can't resist you and your beauty."

"Oh god," She moaned, "I want to feel you lose it with me." She panted, digging her nails into the back of my neck, "Come with me, baby."

"Whatever you want, Mama," I growled, using the new nickname I started experimenting with recently. And she shot off in my lap, coming with pleas and screams as I filled her up, greedily pushing my come into my favorite place on earth.

If she asked me tomorrow to never fill her up again, I'd refuse her. The only thing in life I'd refuse to give to her. Because I couldn't resist it. I craved the feeling of it.

She sagged in my arms, resting her hands on the cushions beneath our knees, and I backed up, letting my cock fall from her body as she sank onto her side as she caught her breath.

Leaning down, I kissed my wife's brow before grabbing the throw blanket off the back of her favorite rocking chair and crawling up onto the bed next to her, pulling her into my side until she rested her head on my chest. I covered us with the blanket and settled into the comfort of her body and the peaceful home I'd built around her.

"I love you." She whispered lazily as she nuzzled deeper, curling in away from the light breeze blowing around us. Even in July, the breeze was chilly in the Utah mountains.

"I love you." I kissed her forehead, covering her up to her shoulders and smiling when she kissed my peck in appreciation. "Do you want to go inside?" The cold air still bothered her, even though she'd lived with me for two years. I was pretty sure it was a trauma response to her time in captivity and following through her escape. It was as if her body remembered and revolted against the memories with each icy breeze. But she never complained, she just snuggled deeper into my embrace when she was chilled.

"Maybe in a little bit." She whispered, running her fingertips through the hair on my chest. "I just want to enjoy this for a few more minutes."

"Whatever you want, darling." I kissed the top of her head and relaxed, knowing exactly what was going to happen to her in a few minutes.

And sure enough, a couple minutes later, the telltale soft hum of her sleeping breath danced across my chest as her body relaxed fully in my arms. Sweet, pretty, and kind, Hadley could nap just about anywhere these days, and I wasn't going to disturb her as long as she was warm and safe.

Well, at least not until right before we needed to leave to get to Mike's for dinner. I'd wake her up with enough time to make her come again and get cleaned up before leaving.

These were the easiest years of our lives, and I was going to let her enjoy them before the baby came and disrupted her easygoing peace.

Epilogue – Hadley

"I don't know about this." I hummed worriedly as Kip buckled the helmet on our son's head.

"What could possibly go wrong, Bambina?" He asked with a sly grin and a wink. He had some grey hair starting around his temples and peppered through his beard, but he was still the most attractive man in the world. It added to his ruggedness and hot dad vibes perfectly.

"Oh, I could think of a few." I deadpanned, rubbing my hands in front of me to fight off the chill.

"C'mon Mama, it'll be fun!" Tyler called out, wiggling his eyebrows under the weight of his bulky snowmobile helmet. "You can ride with me!"

"Not a chance, kiddo." Kip answered for me, "Mama is going to pop your baby sister out any day now and if she rides down this hill, she'll pee her pants."

Little did he know just how soon I'd be popping her out.

I scoffed and ducked my head, rubbing my forehead. "Who says romance is dead, huh?"

Kip smirked at me and then tapped the top of Tyler's helmet, "Let's ride, buddy!"

I watched as Kip loaded our five-year-old son up onto a saucer sled and pushed him to the edge of the hill in front of us. Kip had been sledding at the same hill since he was Tyler's age, but it didn't make my heart beat any slower as my baby sat on the edge of the damn cliff.

Winter sports were fucking weird.

"Hang on tight, Ty!" I yelled and then covered my mouth to keep from screaming as Ty slid off the edge and down the steep, icy hill with his own screams of excitement.

He was going way too fast for my liking, but Kip was right behind him on the snowmobile to pull him back up the steep slope. I shook my head, finally taking a deep breath as my boy came to a stop at the bottom and got off, jumping in the air excitedly.

"Ma-Ma-Ma-Ma."

I turned and my sweet, almost two-year-old son, Dylan, tottered his way toward me through the snow. He looked like an abominable snowman all wrapped up in his winter gear, but I wasn't going to risk him getting frostbite on his tiny toes or fingers as we watched Dad and big brother Ty sledding. Mike and Darla followed close behind Dylan, on their way back with coffee and hot cocoa from the food truck parked in the parking lot.

Like I said, winter sports were weird.

And Utah took their winter sports seriously.

Hence the food truck.

"Hi, baby." I scooped Dylan up and placed him on my hip. Trying not to get emotional about how it may be one of the last times, I picked him up as my youngest little baby. I fought back the normal emotions and pointed down to where Kip had started towing Tyler and a few other kids back up the hill. "You see Daddy?"

"Da-Da-Da." Dylan cheered excitedly for his daddy and brother to return to the top.

"Here you go, dear." Darla handed me a steaming cup of coffee. "It's decaf because I know you're still watching your caffeine intake until little miss gets here."

"God, what I wouldn't give for an espresso." I joked, taking a sip of the coffee, "Thank you, you're too good to me."

"And you're an angel for bringing the boys out today, so close to your due date," Mike added.

I grinned guiltily, "I figured I'd let them have some fun before we locked ourselves away for a few months." I joked, but they all knew that's exactly what we'd do. It was getting to the brutal part of winter where the temperatures were so low at night it hardly even snowed and I was more than ready to hide away at the cabin until spring.

Winter was hard for me. For whatever reason, my body reacted instinctively to the cold and snow, like I had to fight to survive again. It was the biggest scar I had from my kidnapping, and it was one that no one really understood outside of our home, not even my therapist.

My body just couldn't forget how close to dying it had come at the hands of cold Mother Nature I guess, and I wasn't too keen on fighting the inclination to hide away where it was warm for a few months with my cute little family.

Add in the fact that I'd been in silent labor for a few hours already, I was ready to disappear for a while and just soak in the big change coming.

Never mind the fact that the eight-year anniversary of my kidnapping was in a few days too. It was just too much weight on my shoulders to carry all at the same time.

"Do you have any last-minute things you need for the home birth?" Darla asked, eager for another baby to snuggle in her retirement. She would be at the birth, given that she was a retired midwife of many years, but she liked to leave as much prepping as I wanted to us and then would show up with her Mary Poppins purse of goodies and make sure everything went smoothly. She helped deliver both of my boys at home, so I knew I was in excellent hands.

"No, actually, we're all set. Kip has been in go mode for a week or two, so he has already set up and prepped everything, and it's ready to go."

"I just absolutely love seeing this side of him, it never gets old." She smiled warmly at the notion of Kip being sweet and doting.

Mike snorted, "Don't tell him that, he'll have to go split some wood or something to feel manly again."

She swatted her husband lovingly and said something to him, but I missed it as another contraction came, stronger than the others, and I turned away so they wouldn't see me grimace.

Unfortunately, I turned right into Kip as he walked back over to us, carrying Tyler upside down under his arm like a football.

"Hadley?" He put Ty on his feet and cupped my face as I frowned through the pain. "What is it?"

I shook my head, dipping my head and leaning on him as I fought through the pain, and he instantly took over. He held me up and started moving the people and pieces of our life into motion before I even caught my breath to tell him the whole story.

"How long have they been coming?" He asked when I finally took a deep breath and picked my head back up.

"A while." Shyly, I admitted and grimaced as I saw the dark look on his face. I had never hidden labor pains from him before, and he didn't seem impressed with my actions. "I wanted you boys to have today. Before I force everyone to hide because of my own weaknesses."

"Baby," He growled, running his thumbs over my cold cheeks as he stared into my eyes. "Your desire to stay safe and sound in our own world isn't a weakness. It's a coping mechanism and I don't hold that against you, I never have."

"But the kids," I sighed, "Ty wants to go, go, go all the time and—"

But he cut me off, "And he will be just fine, loving on our sweet girls and taking care of you both for a few months." He leaned in and kissed me, as everyone went on around us with their daily lives in a way I envied. "Had, I am aware of the significance of this week, even if you don't want to talk about it. It marks eight years."

"I just don't want you to regret it someday. Regret me if I can't get over it." I hated saying my biggest fears out loud, but I needed to say it in case he really wanted an out.

"For better or worse, darling." He kissed me again and took a deep breath, making me mirror it. "And besides, I was the grumpy recluse when you found me all those years ago, anyway. I fucking love the peace and quiet."

"Da-Da-Da-DA!" Dylan cried out, and I chuckled, knowing peace and quiet weren't in our cards for many years.

I opened my mouth to concede and at least table the discussion for a while when another contraction started, breaking my concentration and making me hum quietly to cope.

"Jesus, honey." He groaned, putting his arms around my waist and gripping my hips in a tight counter-pressure move that relieved the ache. He mastered it during Tyler's labor, and I would have been lost without his support each time.

"That's three minutes apart, Hadley." Darla chimed in, "Mike, take the kids to dinner and then get them a big ice cream cone from Charlie's. My guess is we'll have a baby in a few hours."

"Let's go, give Mama a kiss and hug and tell her what a rockstar she is," Kip said, pulling back as my contraction lessened so Tyler and Dylan could get some love before they ran off with Mike, excited for a dude date and ice cream.

And then Kip picked me up in a bridal carry and got us to the parking lot in record time. When we were almost back home, he reached across the console to take my hand and squeezed it. "Can you believe we're about to have another perfect little baby to love?"

I smiled across the truck to him and tried to let his unmatched happiness calm the anxiety and nerves building inside of me as the contractions got worse and worse. "There's no other way I'd want to live this life,

Kip." He parked the truck and leaned over the console to kiss me, "Thank you for finding me all those years ago."

"Thank you for loving me when I gave you no reason to at all."

Three hours later I laid in bed, nursing our beautiful tiny little baby girl as Kip laid next to me, watching her suckle and explore her new world.

"I can't believe we have a daughter," He whispered, putting his finger against her little hand and smiling when she instantly gripped it. "Daisy would have loved to have a sister."

He often talked about Daisy and Dalton, and even Molly, and it never once felt like he was comparing or second guessing his decisions with me and our family. They were a part of his life and, by extension, a part of our family. Their room was still pink and blue, but we turned it into a toy room for their siblings, keeping their toys and belongings as part of our everyday lives. Their pictures were no longer in boxes, hidden away or locked in grief, they were hung on the walls next to their siblings and we often explained who they were to Tyler when he asked questions.

Three years ago, before I agreed to bear any more of Kip's giant babies, he built a massive addition onto the cabin to accommodate our growing family without losing the space we loved and cherished from his first family.

Our house was a home full of love, laughter, and memories, and it gained another family member that day.

The boys stayed at Mike and Darla's even though I was done laboring early enough for them to come home and meet their baby sister. According to Mike, the sugar high wore off about the time the movie credits rolled for Toy Story and he didn't have the heart to wake them up to bring them home.

Sleepovers were normal for them at Mike and Darla's house, and it warmed my heart knowing my kids had a village of people around them to love them and care for them in ways I never did.

So after my shortest labor yet, in a house devoid of roaring T-Rex characters or singing Mickey Mouse stuffed animals, I basked in the silence and ease with two of my favorite people in the world.

"We have to name her," Kip stated quietly, laying his cheek on my shoulder and nuzzling me. "What do you think about Emma? That one was on the list; do you think it fits?"

"I do, but I think I have one that fits better." I looked away from our beautiful daughter's face to gaze at the man who saved my life in more ways than one. "What do you think about Molly?"

Kip froze and stared back at me as my words processed through his head, "Molly?" He whispered. "Why would you want to name her that?"

He wasn't angry, but I knew my man felt like he was walking on a billion eggshells as he waited for some sort of sign of why I'd recommend naming our daughter after his late wife.

When we first got together and even after we were married, he offered to have her name removed from his tattoos, so that I didn't feel like I was in competition with someone else. A part of him felt guilty, loving two women at once. But I never felt like I had less of him because of it.

So, I refused, strongly, reassuring him I didn't feel lacking to her like I did in the beginning. I knew he loved me. I knew he cherished our life and our family the same way he did theirs, and I knew his position was impossible to be in, so I wouldn't make it harder for him.

I never wanted him to feel like he was living two lives. It was why I had integrated Daisy and Dalton so deeply into our family and life, I just didn't know how to integrate Molly as well.

Until looking into our daughter's beautiful eyes for the first time.

"You've always spoken of Molly's strength and independence. Of how she was a steady wife and mother, holding down her own fort when you were gone and needing no one else." I ran my fingers over his dark beard and smiled at him, "That's exactly the kind of woman I hope our daughter becomes someday. I want her to be resilient and unique in her own way, so she never has to rely on others. I want her to be incredible. And from all the stories you've told, that's exactly who I imagine Molly as. So I think our baby's name should be Molly, to honor your first wife and the mother of our children's siblings. They were the family that taught you how to love and nurture, and today, our children are benefiting from your incredible nature."

"Hadley." He sighed, closing his eyes and resting his forehead against mine as he trembled with emotion. "Our daughter will be strong and resilient because of who *her* mother is. You're the bravest woman I've ever met, and you're also the most loving, kindhearted, and gentle mother. And I love you so fucking much. I don't deserve your brand of love, Hadley Catherine Montgomery. But I hope that someday you understand just how loved you are in return."

Our daughter, Molly, cooed in my arms, drawing our attention back down to her as she stretched and fussed.

"I do, Kip." I kissed her soft forehead and then turned to him for a kiss. "I love you too."

The End.